Dolly Deans of Whitechapel

Patrick Prior

Strumpet Books. London

Contact peoplesplaywright@hotmail.com

Chapter One

<u>London 1899.</u>

"Excuse me, miss, but I must ask you to accompany me to the station."

Dolly Deans felt a jolt of shock as a hand was placed lightly on her shoulder. Turning quickly she caught a glimpse of a blue serge uninform, before looking up to see a smiling young constable looking down at her.

"Thomas Turner, you frightened the life out of me!" she said, jabbing him lightly with a reproving finger. The young policeman's eyes twinkled good-naturedly. "Sorry, Miss Deans, but you're the spitting image of a desperate criminal we're looking for."

Both laughed. Dolly had not seen Thomas since he had left to join the police nearly six months ago. She was taken with how dashing he looked in his uniform. They had been at school together, although he had been two years above. Thomas had always been harum-scarum, up to mischief and playing jokes. He was the last person she thought would be a policeman. But now he looked grown-up and quite impressive.

"What are you doing around these parts, Mr Turner?" she asked, smiling. He put on an expression of mock dignity. "*Constable* Turner 98, if you don't mind," Thomas said, pointing to the police number on his uniform.

Laughingly she said, "To me you'll always be the very naughty boy with the dirty face." The

3

two young people looked at each other. Thomas, now tall and good looking, Dolly, at eighteen, pretty, with a heart-shaped face and lustrous auburn hair. How things had changed from the days in the playground. Both grown and making their way in the world.

The young policeman looked around. "Well, this will be my new beat. Strange to be back here. The streets we played in."

"Are you back living with your mum and dad again?" Dolly asked. Thomas shook his head. "No, I'm living in a police hostel. They like new officers to be close to the station for the first year or so."

Dolly smiled. " So, I expect I'll be seeing you around Whitechapel quite a lot then."

4

"Yes, I expect you will." He winked. " I look forward to that, Dolly Deans." Thomas turned and walked into the milling crowds. She watched him go. He did look very handsome in his uniform.

Dolly made her way along Whitechapel High Street, weaving between the stalls lining the pavements. Dozens of vendors called out in loud voices selling, fruit, fish, clothes and many other types of goods. She felt very tired after being on her feet for ten hours at large shop where she worked.

Turning off the main thoroughfare Dolly walked through a narrow passage which led to the rather shabby street where she lived. Life had been hard since her father died in a shipyard accident three years before, leaving her mother to take care of three children.

Dolly Deans had been the cleverest scholar at the local Board school. Miss Burgess, the headmistress, wanted her to train as a pupil-teacher, but Dolly had to leave to help support the family. However, the teacher still kept in touch with her favourite student and invited her for Sunday tea every so often.

As she reached the entrance she saw a scruffy mongrel sitting on the steps. He didn't have a proper name. Everyone just called him Old Peggy's Dog. Dolly often sat with him, sharing her troubles and secrets.

Sitting down beside the little canine she ruffled him behind the ears. "Hello, Old Peggy's Dog.

6

Have you had a good day?" He looked up at her with soulful eyes, his tail wagging. Dolly smiled. "I wish I had your job. Sitting on these steps all day"

Old Peggy's Dog's mouth was open in a way that he suggested he was grinning. Dolly reached into her bag. "Now, let's see what we've got here." The little dog's tail wagged at a more frantic pace in anticipation. She took out half of a sandwich she had saved from her lunch. "Well, now, bread and a lovely slice of cheese for a lucky little bow-wow."

The sandwich went down in one gulp. Smiling, she patted the dog on the head and went into the entrance of the house. Dolly's family lived on the first floor. Before her father's death they had lived in a pleasant little house, with a garden , in Bethnal Green. But after the tragedy they could not afford the rent and were forced to take three rooms in this tumbledown building.

Opening the door Dolly stepped into the living room. Her mother was at the stove, stirring a pot of soup. Four year old Liza ran to Dolly, arms open. Lifting her little sister up in the air she spun round and round , causing Liza to giggle with delight.

"Hello, mum, that soup smells nice," said Dolly. Mrs Dean smiled wanly. "I managed to get some cheap scrag ends from the butcher. So it should be thick and nourishing." Dolly gazed at her mother. She looked tired and worn from the constant struggle to feed and clothe her family.

"Let me do that, mum, you sit down and have a rest" Dolly said, putting down Liza and hurrying across the room. Mrs Deans smiled gratefully. "Thank you, love, I do feel a bit off colour." She sat down in the sagging armchair by the fire. Dolly was worried. Her mother had never been of the strongest, even at the best of times, but the harshness of their lives seemed to be making her increasingly frail.

"Where's Billy?" Dolly asked as she took a tentative taste of the hot soup. Mrs Deans shrugged. "He went out, said he was going to Spitalfields Market, get some porter work, perhaps."

Dolly was worried about her brother. At fifteen he was aimless. He had left school at the earliest possible opportunity. Billy was no scholar but he was energetic and kind. Despite being desperate for work there seemed to be no opportunities except for casual labouring jobs. He really wanted an apprenticeship of some sort. His mother's biggest worry was that without a decent job he might drift into crime like so many of the young unemployed did in Whitechapel. The temptations to earn easy money was sometimes too overwhelming.

Stepping away from the stove Dolly began laying out plates and spoons. From the cupboard she took the remaining half of a loaf and placing it on a bread-board cut it into thick slices. When she was finished she called her mother and Liza to the table.

As they began to eat, dipping the bread into the thick soup, Dolly nodded over to a huge pile of matchboxes on the dresser.

"I see you managed to finish those, mum." Grimacing, Mrs Deans said, "Not as much as I'd hoped love. They only pay threepence a hundred. Still, every little helps, eh?"

Making matchboxes was a cottage industry in the east end. Many poor women worked long hours at home gluing hundreds together for a pittance.

"Guess who I saw today, mum?" Dolly said, reaching for another slice of bread. Mrs Deans shook her head. "Well, I'm sure I wouldn't know in a hundred thousand guesses. So you'd better tell me." Dolly smiled. Her mother's

11

reply was something her father used to say. "Thomas Turner."

The older woman's eyes widened in surprise. "Little Tommy Turner? Well, I never."

"He's not so little now," Dolly said as she broke the bread into smaller pieces for Liza. "He's a policeman and six foot tall if he's an inch." Her mother raised her eyebrows in surprise. " A policeman? Who'd have thought it, and him such a little tyke when he was a boy."

They both laughed at this. After the meal was over Dolly washed up and prepared Liza for bed. When the little girl had settled down Mrs Deans sat on one side of the fire, mending a tear in Billy's trousers, while Dolly sat on the other side reading a book she had borrowed from Miss

Burgess. Finally, with a yawn, the older woman went to bed.

Dolly sat by the firelight. She would wait up for Billy, not able to rest until he was home safely. Despite trying to concentrate on her book her thoughts kept straying to Thomas. He did look very dashing in that uniform.

Chapter Two

Dolly stared at herself in the mirror for a moment and then nodded. "Well, Miss Deans, I think I can say we're presentable." She said this aloud to the empty room. Her mother had taken Liza to visit a cousin in Shoreditch, while Billy was off playing football.

She enjoyed the luxury of having the house to herself for a little while. It was Sunday, her only day off. With her best dress on, and a lovely hat her mother had made her, she was off to meet her best friend, Millie Ryan, for a walk in Victoria Park.

Hurrying along the High Street she could see crowds of people dressed in their Sunday best heading for the park. The sun was out and even

Whitechapel looked bright and jolly. Reaching Millie's house she rapped loudly on the knocker. Almost immediately the door swung open. Her friend answered and, like her, was done up in her best clothes.

"In you come, Dolly, nearly ready, won't be a mo." Millie said cheerfully.   Dolly stepped inside. She had been coming to the house for years. She and Millie were in the same class all through school. Her friend was not academic but she was shrewd and quick-witted, qualities much needed in Whitechapel.

In the living room Millie's father and mother were deep in the Sunday papers. Dolly called out to them. "Hello, Mrs Ryan, hello, Mr Ryan." Both mumbled replies before resuming their reading of the latest scandals. "Here, Dolly, come here, have a look," Millie said gesturing over to the kitchen table. "What do you think?"

The table was covered with two trays of brightly coloured cakes. Tarts, sponges, and buns. Dolly's eyes widened in amazement. "Millie, where did these come from?" Her friend grinned proudly. "I made them." " *You* made them? But how? Why?"

The girl shrugged. " I read this book by a woman called Mrs Beeton. It had all these recipes. And I thought, right, I could make these. I could sell these."

Dolly shook her head. "Sell them? Where?" Her friend laughed incredulously. "Where do you think, silly, in the market."

"But you don't have a stall," said Dolly. Millie waved away her objection. " I don't need a stall to start with. I start with a tray; like the pedlars have. And then after a while I'll get a stall and after that a shop and after that lots of shops!"

Dolly clapped in delight at her friend's boldness "That's a wonderful idea, Millie. You really think you can do it?" Millie Ryan nodded. " Course. Other people do it and they aint no smarter than me."

The two friends ate a cake each and then made their way to the park. As they drew nearer the crowds grew denser. It seemed as if the whole of the east end was there. Victoria Park was perhaps the only green area many would see. Dolly and Millie, arm in arm, walked through

17

the gates. They were met by the sound of a brass band playing somewhere in the distance.

The sun beat down and the ice cream vendors were swamped by perspiring strollers. As they passed under the cooling shade of a grove of trees Dolly suddenly saw a tall, blue-clad figure walking towards them. It was Thomas. He spotted them at the same time and broke into a broad grin.

"Oh my, and what do we have here, two trouble makers, I'll be bound." The friends laughed. Millie looked Thomas up and down. "Who would have thought it, Tommy Turner, a guardian of the Law. I remember you filching apples off old Mr Simpsons fruit stall."

"Ssshhh. Let's keep that between ourselves, eh?" he said with a broad wink. Dolly could see his face was red and thought he must be hot under the heavy blue serge uniform and tight collar.

"You look as if you're ready to melt, Thomas. Can we tempt you with an ice-cream?" The tall policeman shook his head, "I'd like nothing better, Dolly, but I must uphold the dignity of the Law. Suppose I have to suddenly chase some miscreant. How would it look if I had a truncheon in one hand and an ice-cream cornet in the other?"

The girls burst into laughter at this. Thomas looked at their finery. "You two look smart enough to meet the queen." Millie put on an exaggerated posh voice "Yes, as a matter of fact we're just on our way to the palace now, doncha know."

At this Thomas glanced across to where crowds gathered at the lake. "Oh, oh, I see my sergeant looking at me. He doesn't seem pleased at me chatting. Better be off. See you ladies later." As he started to move off he turned. "By the way, there's a dance at Bow Church next Saturday, are you two going?"

Dolly shook her head " I didn't know about it. Did you, Millie?"

"I do now," said Millie. " Will you be there, Constable Turner?" Thomas smiled. "If you two promise to be there. I don't want to be a wallflower." Millie affected an nonchalant air.

"Maybe we will, we'll have to check our social diaries, my good man."

He turned to Dolly. "Will you be there, Miss Deans? I'd like it if you were." Dolly felt her face turn bright red. "Well...if...Millie...we'll see." He looked deep into her eyes. "I really would like to see you there." At this the young policeman walked smartly away.

Millie's eyes widened and she whistled softly. "Well, well, well, I think someone has an admirer" Dolly felt herself blush again. "What? Oh, don't be silly. He was just being friendly, Millie." Her friend chuckled. "Yes, *sweetheart* friendly. I think Tommy Turner has a fancy for you, my girl." "That's enough," she said, giving her friend a playful push, "Let's have an ice cream."

They walked arm in arm to one of the little carts and after a wait bought two cornets. Sitting on a bench under the cool shade of an oak tree they discussed Millie's plans for her cake empire. Dolly was happy for her friend, but was only half-listening at times. Her thoughts kept turning to Thomas and the way her looked at her when he said he would really like to see her at the dance.

It was strange. They had been childhood friends and had she never thought that he might think of her in that way. In turn, Dolly felt feelings stir in her. He was no longer to her Thomas Turner, a mischievous school-friend, he was a handsome young man to whom she was drawn.

When Millie had finished telling her plans they both sat quietly looking at the colourful scene before them. Children ran back and forth, people laughed and joked. Ladies paraded their finery. Dolly wished the east end could be like this all the time. Instead of being a grim, relentless struggle.

She kept looking hopefully for glimpse of Thomas but to her disappointment there was no sign of him. Finally she turned to Millie. "So, do you want to go to this dance on Saturday?" she said, with an attempt at a nonchalant tone. "Do you?" Millie Ryan asked, grinning widely.

Dolly shrugged slightly. "I'm not really bothered either way. But as he asked us, I suppose it would only be polite to go". After a short break she added, "Just to be sociable, of course."

At this her friend broke into a hearty laugh. "Yeah, just to be *sociable* of course."

Chapter Three

Dolly pulled the bell-chord and began to walk down the winding tram stairs. It was Monday morning and the jollity of Sunday in the park seemed a lifetime away. The shop where she worked, Wentlock's, was in the west end, just off Oxford Street.

She had been there for nearly six months. Although Dolly quite liked most of the people she worked with, the hours were long and the customers sometimes very demanding. Also Miss Meredith, the manageress, ruled the place with a rod of iron. Like the other girls, Dolly was always uneasy when her gimlet glare fell on her.

Stepping off the tram she looked up at the clock on the front of an office building and saw

25

she was twenty minutes early. Lateness was the most serious offence of all in Miss Meredith's eyes. Any girl late more than once in a month was instantly dismissed. As her family depended on her wages Dolly could not afford to lose her position.

The morning was sunny and, as she had some time to kill, Dolly decided to sit in a little public garden set out in front of a row of grand houses near the shop. She thought it would give her a chance to think again about Thomas. She had thought of little else since the meeting in the park.

Crossing the road she noticed a fashionably-dressed, middle-aged woman seem to totter and hold on to the railings surrounding the garden.

Dolly immediately ran over and took her lightly by the elbow.

"Are you alright, ma'am? Can I help?" The woman looked dazed. Taking a deep breath she gripped Dolly's supporting arm tightly. "Thank you, my dear," she gasped. "I feel a little faint. I wonder could you help me to one of those benches?"

Gently guiding her to a seat Dolly helped the lady sit down. It was obvious she had suffered some sort of turn. Her face was white and her hands shook. Dolly knelt down and looked at her concernedly. " Is there anything I can do, ma'am? Shall I fetch a doctor?" The woman shook her head and tried a weak smile. "No, no doctor, my dear. I have foolishly forgotten my pills. My own fault. I just need to rest for a few minutes"

Dolly suddenly recognised her. It was Mrs Markham. She often came into the shop. The other girls thought she was rather too grand and called her the 'Duchess' behind her back. It was obvious by the quality of her clothes and the way she spoke she was from the upper-classes. But, sitting there, she looked frail and vulnerable.

Holding her hand Dolly said "Perhaps a glass of water might help, ma'am?' The lady nodded weakly in agreement. Hurrying across the road Dolly went into the chemist shop opposite and explained the situation. Returning with the water she handed it to Mrs Markham. Sitting down beside the older woman Dolly watched solicitously as she took a drink.

"Little sips, ma'am. That's the best way." The stricken woman smiled weakly. "You seem to know what to do. Are you a nurse?" Dolly laughed. "No, ma'am, but I have a family and there's always some ailment to deal with. My mother is prone to slight fainting fits too, Mrs Markham."

Placing the glass on the bench Mrs Markham looked closely at Dolly. " You say my name. Do I know you, child?" Dolly smiled. " You may have seen me, ma'am, I work behind the counter at Wentlock's." The woman looked more closely at her. "Yes, I remember you now. You sold me something recently." Dolly nodded. "Yes, three yards of red silk ribbon and a lace veil."

Mrs Markham chuckled and applauded lightly. "My goodness, what a memory. You are to be congratulated." Dolly noticed the colour had returned to her face and her hands had stopped shaking. "Do you enjoy working there?" she asked. Shrugging her shoulders Dolly said, "It's hard work, ma'am, but some of the time it can be nice."

Glancing over at the clock. Dolly saw she had just under five minutes before her starting time. She was anxious to be on her way but felt she couldn't leave Mrs Markham until she knew the lady was alright. Almost as if she could read the younger girl's mind Mrs Markham patted her shoulder. "Now, my dear, I won't detain you any longer. You mustn't be late."

Satisfying herself that the woman seemed to have recovered, Dolly stood up. "Well, if you are sure you can get home by yourself, ma'am." Mrs Markham pointed across the gardens. "I shall be fine, my dear. I don't have far to go. I live in that house over there, the one with the green door. Now you be off."

Giving her a brief smile, Dolly turned to go. Mrs Markham called her back. Fumbling in her purse she said, "Here, I must give you something for your trouble." Dolly shook her head decisively. "Oh, no Mrs Markham. I don't want anything. Not for helping someone."

The older woman looked askance at Dolly for a few seconds. "What's your name, child?" "Dolly Deans, ma'am." Mrs Markham squeezed her hand. "Well, Dolly Deans, you are a credit to your parents. Thank you for all your kindness. I shall not forget it."

After returning the glass to the chemists, Dolly rushed to the shop. The clock said she had less than two minutes. Hurrying inside she was met with a frosty glare by the ferocious Miss Meredith, who pointedly made a show of checking her watch.

Her lips pursed in disapproval. " Nearly late, Deans." Dolly looked up at the large clock on the wall. "But not *quite*, Miss Meredith. Just on time," she said with a hint of defiance in her voice. This brought a scowl to the face of the manageress, who did not like anyone answering back. Dolly rushed to the counter, lifted out her work pinafore and began to place various goods on the glass top for display.

Walking over to the counter Mrs Meredith stared at her for a moment. Then a vindictive smile formed on her thin lips.

"Oh, Deans, I shan't need you at the counter today." Dolly felt a chill of fear. Surely she was not going to be dismissed. That would not be fair. She had not been late. The manageress grinned. It reminded Dolly of the smile of a crocodile she had seen at the zoo.

"The goods in the old basement need to be sorted, counted and listed today. We have stocktaking next week. Be so good as to take a clip-board, a pencil and a lantern and see to it, will you?" Dolly's heart sank. The old basement had not been used for years. It was dark and hidden under inches of dirt and dust. She knew that any stock down there was water-damaged or obsolete. This was Miss Meredith's petty spite.

Sighing, she came out from behind the counter. "Yes, Miss Meredith." Dolly headed for the store room to collect a lantern and clip-board under the iron glare of the vindictive manageress. Dolly held up the items. "I'm ready, Miss Meredith." The older woman smirked. "Good, now off you go." As the despondent Dolly moved away, the manageress called after her. "Oh, and by the way, Deans, do be careful. There are rats. They tend to bite."

After lighting the lantern Dolly unlocked the creaking door, which had obviously had not been opened for months. She made her way down the stairs, brushing cobwebs out of her hair and off her face. Here, at the bottom, she faced shelves stacked with dusty, mouldering boxes.

Her heart sank. This would take a whole day. And all for no useful purpose, apart from satisfying Miss Meredith's vindictiveness. If only Mrs Markham hadn't have taken poorly then this wouldn't have happened. Not that she regretted helping. It just seemed unfair. Dolly remembered something she had heard once. *No good deed goes unpunished.* At the time she thought it didn't make sense, but now she knew exactly what it meant.

Sighing, she began the count the first row of dusty boxes.

Chapter Four

"Oh, my goodness, love. Where have you been? Working down the coal-mines?" Mrs Deans looked at the state of Dolly as she came in the door. She had smudges on her face and hands and straggles of cobwebs trailing from her hair. Baby Liza looked up at her and gurgled with laughter.

Dolly had done her best to clean up before she left the shop, but Miss Meredith made sure she stayed in the basement until the very last minute. So she only had time to give her face and hands a cursory wipe at the sink. She had felt horribly embarrassed on the tram, aware people were staring. Going over to the mirror she contemplated her dishevelled state.

"Look at me. I'm like the Wreck of the Hesperus. That horrible Miss Meredith, mum, she made me work in a filthy basement all day," Dolly said, as she licked her finger and wiped a spot of dirt from her brow. Mrs Deans shook her head. "Whatever would she do that for?" Hanging her coat on a nail on the back of the door, Dolly scowled. "Because she's a very spiteful person and I don't think she likes me."

Mrs Deans put out the remains of the soup and bread from a few days before on the table. "Now, you never mind, love. You have something to eat and have a rest."

"I have to wash properly, mum. When I've eaten I'll go round the public bath houses in Castle alley, have a nice long hot soak." She looked down at Liza. "And what are you smiling at you cheeky thing? What's so funny?" The little girl giggled as Dolly tickled her.

Washing her hands in the small sink she joined her mother and Liza at the table. Just as they began to eat the door opened and Billy came in. He looked at the food.

"I'm starving. Leave some for me." Walking over to the table he sat down. Mrs Deans frowned at him. "Look at your hands, William Deans. Filthy. You go and wash them right now."

Rolling his eyes in exasperation Billy moaned. "But, mum!' However his mother's implacable stare sent him to the sink where he gave his hands a quick rinse before he joined them at the table.

Billy frowned. "Soup again? Can't we have a nice bit of meat for a change?" Dolly grinned. "Yes, we could eat like the Lord Mayor of London if we had the money, Billy Deans, but we don't so be grateful for what you've got."

Her brother looked at her more closely. "Here, Dolly, do you know your face is dirty?" Dolly widened her eyes in mock surprise. "You don't say!" At this mother and daughter laughed heartily. Liza joined in although she didn't know why she was laughing.

Dolly held out her hand. "By the way, speaking of money, let's have some." Billy squirmed in protest. "I've only got a shilling and

I need that." Pointing to the table, she said, "You see that bread, you see that soup, do you think they're all brought by the magical food-fairy. No, they all had to be paid for. Almost all of my wages go in rent and food, and clothes. You're part of this family, Billy Deans, you have to pay your share. So cough up."

Reluctantly Billy handed over the coin to Dolly who then passed it to her mother. They ate in silence for a few seconds before Mrs Deans spoke. "Any chance of work, Billy?" Shaking his head the boy said "No, mum, just casual in the market. Although, when I passed, Mrs Pemberton said she might have some work for me."

Dolly and her mother exchanged concerned glances. Mrs Pemberton owned the local haberdashers, but it was common knowledge around Whitechapel that she also dealt in stolen goods. The police had suspected her for some time but could never find proof. She was especially clever at creating an image of outer respectability, prominent in helping charitable causes and was even on the board of an orphanage.

Staring hard at her brother, Dolly pointed a warning finger. "You stay away from Hannah Pemberton, Billy Deans." The boy grinned. "Don't you worry about me, sis, I know what's what." "You know what I mean, Billy," his sister said sternly, "now you promise you won't do any work for her." Taking a spoonful of soup the young man nodded a reluctant acquiescence.

After the meal Dolly put on her coat. As she left she told to Billy clear up. Hurrying through Whitechapel she soon arrived at the new public bath houses in Castle Alley . The facilities had been a boon to all who lived in the district. They provided endless hot water for laundering and bathing. Dolly used the baths at least three times a week.

Walking inside she was enveloped in a cloud of soapy steam and the smell of carbolic. Going to the booth she booked into one of the slipper baths. Ten minutes later she was luxuriating up to her neck in hot soapy water. Lying in a dreamy half-state Dolly let all the tiredness and exhaustion of the day melt away. Millie had given her a bottle of rose water at Christmas. Added to the bath it filled the chamber with a delicious scent of summer.

Dolly could have stayed there forever, but after a while the water began to cool. Dressing, she left the bath house, feeling fresh and clean again after her day in the basement. As she made her way home her thoughts turned, as they had so many times in the last few days, to Thomas and the dance on Saturday. Despite keeping a keen eye out for him on patrol, Dolly had never managed to spot the young policeman. The week had seemed endless and it seemed Saturday night would never come.

As she passed the London Hospital. She heard a bawling voice which sounded very familiar. Dolly then laughed with surprise when she saw Millie, with a tray full of cakes, selling her wares. She rushed over to her friend.

"Millie Ryan! As I live and breathe. You're doing it." Her friend gave a cheerful grin. 'Course I am. Told you I would." Dolly could see she had decorated her tray with brightly coloured streamers and tinsel. It looked jolly and would certainly catch people's attention.

Delightedly Dolly clapped her friend on the shoulder. "That's amazing. How are you doing?" Pointing into the tray Millie said," Have a look." Looking in Dolly could see there was only a few of pastries left. "Nearly sold out," the young baker said proudly.

At that moment a man stopped and asked for a bun. "That will be tuppence please," Millie said with a professional flourish. As the customer walked away the friends exchanged smiles. Dolly shook her head in admiration. " I'm so proud of you, Millie, you are so clever. Have you made much money?" Millie looked around before taking out a little velvet bag. She shook it. A jingle of coins sounded. "Three shillings today."

Dolly let out an impressed soundless whistle. "Three shillings? For just one day? I only earn fifteen shillings for a whole week." "You look like a shiny new penny. Where have you been?"

Millie   said, taking in her friend's freshly scrubbed face and tousled hair.

"The bath house. Rotten day at work." Millie gave her shoulder a sympathetic squeeze. "Never mind, Dolly. Have a cake. In fact take those ones, they're a bit stale now" She pointed to four rather sad –looking sponge squares in the corner of the tray. Lifting them out Dolly carefully wrapped   the   cakes   in   her handkerchief. "Thanks, Mill, I'll take them home as a treat for Liza and mum."

  Walking   along   the   High   Street   Millie occasionally called out her wares. As they passed Whitechapel underground station a newspaper seller bawled out the headlines. By his side was a placard which said *War Clouds Gather.*

Turning to her friend Dolly said, "Here, you see that, Mill? Do you think there's going to be a war?" Millie snorted in derision. "Course, not. Just newspapers. They'll say anything to sell. Who would want to fight us, anyway?"

Finally they reached the corner where Dolly turned off.

"Well, Millie Ryan," Dolly said standing back and looking her friend up and down, "I do believe you are going to get those shops someday." Her friend smiled. "And you can come in and eat for free." They both laughed.

"So? Dolly asked, arching her eyebrows. Grinning, Millie affected innocence "So?"

"You know what I mean, Miss Ryan. The dance on Saturday. Are we going, yes or no?" "Of course we are," Millie said chuckling, "but just to be *sociable* course."

Dolly left her friend and made her way through the alleyway to her street. Sitting on the steps, as usual, was Old Peggy's Dog. When the little canine saw her he sat up and looked at her expectantly. She patted his head.

"Hello, Old Peggy's Dog. Another busy day?" He turned his head on one side, looking at her quizzically Then his brown eyes darted to Dolly's bag. His tongue lolled open expectantly. She stroked his head gently and leaned closer. "I know what you want, you greedy little bow-wow." Opening her handkerchief she took out one of the stale cakes. Throwing it high she clapped as Old Peggy's Dog leap and caught it in mid-air.

"Bravo! You clever dog. Now, I've got to go. But before I do I have a secret to tell you, but you've got to promise to keep it between us." As he stared at her Dolly was almost convinced the scruffy canine understood every word she said. Leaning closer she whispered to the little dog. "I think Thomas likes me" Lowering her voice even further she said "And I like him too, very, very much."

Chapter Five

"Hold still, for goodness sake, girl!" Mrs Deans looked sharply at Dolly as she tried to pin the bottom of her dress. Baby Liza watched fascinated as her older sister stood on a chair, having last minute adjustments made to her gown.

The week had seemed endless. Each day an eternity. Dolly had never watched the clock so much, wishing the time away. She was so excited at the prospect of seeing Thomas at the dance that even Miss Meredith's unpleasant behaviour could not dim her spirits.

Her mother was a clever needlewoman, taking one of Dolly's old dresses and, after sponging it

51

clean, had added ribbons and replaced the buttons so that it now looked very pretty.

With a final check, Mrs Deans stood back and pronounced herself satisfied. "I think you might do, I think you might just well do." Stepping down Dolly went to the full- length mirror on the inside door of the wardrobe. She stared at her herself for a few seconds then whirled round, checking the back. "Oh, mum," she said joyfully, "it's lovely, it's the loveliest dress in London. In the world!"

Mrs Deans laughed. "Well, maybe in Whitechapel at least." At that moment Liza, with outstretched arms ran towards Dolly. Seeing her little sister's grubby fingers reaching for her she let out a yell of alarm. "No, Liza, no!

Mum!" Just as Liza was about to grab the dress, Mrs Deans caught the child and whisked her away. Dolly sighed with relief.

At that moment the door opened and Billy came in. He looked at Dolly and whistled. "Well, I'll be blowed, no one told me Queen Vicky was coming to tea! I'd have worn me best bib and tucker." His mother shook her finger in mock warning. "That's enough cheek from you, young man. And by the way, less of the Queen Vicky, if you don't mind. A bit more respect for her majesty. It's Queen Victoria to you."

Billy bowed. "Oh, I'm s hawfully sorry, mater. Please convey my most humble apologies the next time you're at the palace."

His mother laughed. "Cheeky rascal," she said, ruffling his hair.. Dolly stood in the middle of the room. "So, Billy, what do you think?" The boy made an elaborate play of studying her carefully for a moment. "You know what I think, sis, I think you look like...like a dying duck in a thunderstorm." Dolly's eyes widened with mock outrage. "Well, that's very nice, I must say." Her brother grinned "Only joking, sis, you look lovely. You could give Marie Lloyd a run for her money any day."

Dolly smiled at the compliment and looking in the mirror began to brush her hair. Billy handed his mother some coins. "What's this?" she said, staring in surprise. "Two shillings? Where did this come from?" Her son shrugged casually. "Got paid for carrying some stuff." Mrs Deans looked at him more closely. "What stuff? Who for?"

"Mrs Pemberton." Dolly turned sharply. "You know what we said about Hannah Pemberton, Billy. You were told to keep away from her." The boy dismissed her objections with a wave of his hand. "It wasn't anything illegal, honest. Only helped the delivery man carry a few crates into the shop." His mother shot him a warning look. "Well, you make it the last time."

At that moment there was a knock at the door. Mrs Dean opened it to find Millie Ryan there, arrayed in her finery. "Come in, Millie." The girl stepped into the room and twirled around. "Well, what do you think?" Dolly and her mother made appreciative noises. "You look lovely, Millie. A real treat for the eyes," Dolly said, looking at her friends appearance . Millie made a curtsy of appreciation. Billy stared at both of them and smiled. "Two toffs in the house, now I know Queen Vicky must be expected." His mother flicked his ear lightly, causing him to yelp. "What did I tell you already, young man. A bit of respect for our queen."

Millie put a little box she was carrying on the table. "This is for you, Mrs Deans." Dolly's mother opened the container to see an assortment of buns and cakes. Her eyes widened in delight. "Oh, Millie, dear, that is so kind. But you shouldn't have."

The young baker smiled. "Just a few I had left over. Didn't want them to go to waste." Dolly knew the cakes were not left over. They were fresh. She was touched by her friend's kindness. Billy made a grab for a cake. His mother slapped his hand away.

"You wash your hands first, young man. And then we'll all sit and have tea and cake, like proper toffs."

As Dolly finished brushing hair, her family sat at table. Each took a cake and Mrs Dean poured the tea. Millie laughed as she saw that baby Liza had managed get cream all over her face immediately. Even her eyebrows were coated.

After saying their goodbyes, both girls left with Mrs Deans warnings about being careful and being home by ten o'clock ringing in their ears. The dance was at Bow Church which was at about a mile walk. But the evening was warm and sunny and the friends chatted happily about their week. Millie was doing well and told Dolly if things kept going the way they had it wouldn't be too long until she could afford to rent a stall.

Arriving at the church hall they paid their threepence, which entitled them to a cup of tea and a cake. The venue was already crowded with young people. All dressed in their finery. At one end of the room a three piece band struck up an energetic version of 'Boiled Beef and Carrots.'

The hall was draped in colourful streamers. Bunting was hung across the stage where the musicians played. To Dolly it seemed as if the whole of the east end was there. She and Millie waved to people they knew.

Both the girls drew appreciative glances from the young single men dotted around the edge of the hall. The band struck up a polka and the floor was filled with prancing, energetic dancers. Going to a serving hatch, situated in one wall, Dolly and Millie exchanged their tickets for a cup of tea and a cake.

Sitting down they watched the dancers while sipping tea and delicately nibbling at their cakes. Millie's nose wrinkled in disgust. "Call this a cake? What did they use? Sawdust and cough

59

mixture? If I sold cakes like this I should be out of business in no time."

Dolly laughed as her friend made a great show of putting the cake back on the hatch- cover with a look of disgust on her face. The polka finished and, as the dancers cleared the floor, Dolly looked around to see if she could spot Thomas. There was no sign. She turned to Millie. "Can't see Thomas, can you?" Her friend shook her head. "No, but it's early, Dolly. He might be just finishing duty." This comforted Dolly Deans a little bit. But every time the door of the hall opened, she looked at it, her heart beating with anticipation.

As the music struck up again two young men approached and asked them to dance. Dolly shook her head, but Millie accepted and was soon whirling around the floor in a waltz. She was a good dancer and cut an elegant figure as she swept around the room.

At one point Dolly saw a tall figure come through the door she stood up expectantly, but then felt a bitter pang of disappointment as she realised it was not Thomas.

The evening wore on and Dolly became more anxious and disappointed. Millie tried to cheer her up and even persuaded her to dance occasionally with some of the young men who asked. But her heart wasn't in it. Eventually Dolly sat like a wallflower .

Millie had no shortage of partners and danced most of the evening away. Between dances her efforts to cheer the friend up fell flat. At half past nine it was announced the band's last number of the evening would be. 'After the Ball.'

When the bandleader sang the line, 'many the hopes that have vanished, after the ball' Dolly thought her heart would break. It took all her courage not to cry. How could Thomas let her down like this?

Millie could see how distressed her friend was and tried to put forward some possible, unlikely, reasons for Thomas's non-appearance. But she was only going through the motions and said them without any real conviction.

The walk home was almost silent. Millie tried to cheer Dolly up but her efforts were only met with monosyllabic answers. At the corner of the road, Millie hugged her friend.

"Don't you worry, Dolly, plenty more fish in the sea."

They parted ways. Now that she was alone Dolly let the tears trickle down her cheeks. She could not believe Thomas could do this, not after the way he looked into her eyes.

Reaching the steps a familiar figure sat up. Old Peggy's Dog, looked at her expectantly. Dolly sighed and sat down. "I'm sorry, bow-wow, no food today." She patted his head. "You're lucky. All you need is enough to eat and a place to sleep."

Wrapping her arms around the little dog's neck she leaned against him. "I'm so sad, Old

Peggy's Dog. I thought he liked me. I thought he

liked me, I really did."

Chapter Six

Dolly had had a restless and unhappy night. She had been devastated at being stood up by Thomas, never thinking he was that type of chap. Now, standing waiting for the tram, she tried to compose herself for another day of facing Miss Meredith.

The sun was blazing down, even at that early hour. Dolly wished she could just walk somewhere green and quiet and be alone with her thoughts. Suddenly she saw a blue-clad figure hurrying towards her. It was Thomas! Her heart beat faster. The young policeman reached her and put his arm on her shoulder.

"Dolly, thank goodness I found you." She looked at him coldly. "I don't think we have anything to say, Thomas Turner." He stared into her eyes, his face a mask of misery. "Please, listen. I couldn't help what happened. I was dressed and ready to leave my room when the sergeant came and said I was needed for emergency duty."

Trying to look cynical, but failing completely, Dolly looked up and him. " Emergency duty? You expect me to swallow a tall tale like that? You left me waiting like a fool. I don't think we have anything more to say to each other, do you?"

Taking her hand he said, "Please, Dolly, I give you my solemn word I'm speaking the truth." He took a deep breath. " There was an outbreak of trouble at Aldgate last night. Gangs of hooligans were fighting and causing damage.

Police reinforcements were needed urgently. Everyone in the hostel was summoned. I had to go right away. I didn't have a chance to let you know."

Dolly could see his upset was genuine. He looked tired. She felt her resolve weaken. "Why didn't you come afterwards?" Thomas gave a wry grin. "I've just come off duty. We were there all night." He touched her cheek tenderly. "Dolly, I think you know how I feel about you. I would never let you down deliberately, surely you know that?"

She felt a wave of relief sweep through her. All her doubts about Thomas melted away. Dolly smiled at him sympathetically. "You look very tired." The young policeman nodded. "A bit. I need a sleep. But telling you first what happened was the most important thing."

She could see the tram coming. She said "I have to go." Squeezing her hand he said "I'll see you later. I thought we might go to the music hall this Saturday, if you like." Dolly returned the pressure on his fingers. "I would like that very much, Thomas."

Stepping onto the platform Dolly waved to him until the vehicle turned a corner. Taking a seat she felt light-hearted again. Let Miss Meredith do her worst, she had a sweetheart.

Dolly made the journey with a little half-smile on her face. She could see people looking at her but she didn't care. Two men, sitting opposite, discussed the growing possibility of war. But

Dolly Deans was falling in love and in no mood for depressing news.

Stepping off the tram she almost skipped into the shop. Dolly called a cheery good morning to Miss Meredith. In return the sour-faced manageress shot her a scowl. Going to her counter she put on her pinafore and, as usual, laid out items for display on the glass top.

The shop was busy and she was surprised to find that the next time she looked up at the clock it was almost lunch-time. Dolly decided as the day was so nice she would eat in the gardens. She knew that Miss Meredith thought that leaving the shop during the day was a minor act of betrayal. But Dolly Deans was too happy to let this worry her.

After storing some stock under the counter Dolly looked up to see Miss Meredith speaking to a well-dressed customer, whom she immediately recognised. It was Mrs Markham. She could hear what they said quite clearly.

"So, you understand what I need?" Miss Meredith rubbed her hands together unctuously. "Of course, Mrs Markham. Anything you require, Mrs Markham. Just let us know how we can serve you best, Mrs Markham."

Dolly had to hide a smile at the manageress' grovelling manner as she spoke. Mrs Markham nodded. "Yes, well, I'm planning to freshen my soft furnishings. I should like samples of covering material, ribbons and lace brought to the house. And someone to advise me perhaps on the best combinations."

At this Miss Meredith bobbed obsequiously several times "Of course, Mrs Markham. That would be our pleasure, Mrs Markham. I will be glad to do it myself, at your earliest convenience of course, Mrs Markham."

"Thank you so much, Miss Meredith, but I think that young lady might suit me best." As she said this Mrs Markham pointed across to Dolly. The manageress' eyes bulged with surprise and disbelief. "That girl? But she has only been with us a short while, Mrs Markham. I do not think she has the experience or expertise you need. With the greatest respect, I think perhaps, in this case, I might be the better choice"

Edith Markham smiled and shook her head. "Thank you, I do appreciate the offer, but I found that any time I've had dealings with her that young lady was very efficient and helpful. Please send her over with the samples, shall we say, two o'clock this afternoon?"

With a sickly grin Miss Meredith nodded a reluctant acquiescence. "Of course, Mrs Markham, two o' clock it shall be." After seeing her customer to the door, the manageress turned to Dolly, her face like thunder. Stomping up to the counter she glared at the younger girl. "You heard the customer, Deans," she hissed through compressed lips, " later make up a sample case. You shall take it over at two o'clock."

"Yes, Miss Meredith," Dolly said quietly. She had to fight down the impulse to smile at the manageress' discomfiture. But she knew one hint of amusement would probably lead to instant dismissal.

The rest of the morning passed in an icy and uncomfortable atmosphere as Miss Meredith took her anger out on Dolly and the other assistants, snapping at them as she found fault at every turn. It was a relief to Dolly when her lunch -break came and she was able to escape the poisonous mood of the shop and sit under the trees, eating her sandwiches.

Thoughts of Thomas filled her head. She was so relieved that he had not let her down. His distress at not meeting her at the dance was obvious. Even after a night on duty he had rushed to explain. She was excited at the thought of going with him to the music hall. Dolly had not been since before her father died. They used to go as a family every Saturday night. She always loved the music and colour and laughter.

Checking the clock on the wall of a business building she saw that she only had five minutes of her lunch-time left. So lost in thought had she been with dreams of herself and Thomas that time had slipped past so fast.

As she stood up she wondered why Mrs Markham had chosen her to bring the samples. After all, Miss Meredith was right, she was a very junior assistant. But, for whatever her reason, Dolly was looking forward to a break in the daily routine.

Making her way back to Wentlock's she slipped on her pinafore and began serving customers. Just after one 'o clock the manageress came over. "Well, Deans, you'd better start making up that sample case now. And make sure you only include our deluxe goods. None of the cheaper materials." She leaned forward. "Mrs Markham is a very important customer, and very rich, so you will give her first class service, or else find yourself another position. Do I make myself clear?" Dolly nodded. "Yes, Miss Meredith."

Taking a tray she began to choose a variety of goods she thought might suit. Miss Meredith had told her only to select the most expensive items, but Dolly had no intention of cheating Mrs Markham. She was a nice lady and deserved to be treated with respect and honesty.

Finally Dolly was satisfied that the goods she had in the sample case were the best selection possible. She made her way to the front door, hoping Miss Meredith wouldn't want to inspect the contents. The manageress was at the other end of the shop, so thanking her lucky stars Dolly Deans crossed the road and made for the grand house Edith Markham had pointed out the day she had taken ill.

Taking a deep breath Dolly walked up the steps and rang the bell. After a moment a maid answered. " Hrrrmm" she said, nervously clearing her throat, " I'm from Wentlock's. Mrs Markham is expecting me."

The maid indicated that she step inside. Closing the door the servant told her to wait. Left alone in the hall, Dolly gazed around in awe To her it was like a palace. Deep carpets, elegant furniture. A high ceiling, with a huge chandelier which sent out sparkles of light. Dolly had never seen a place so beautiful. This was a long way from life in Whitechapel. Her thoughts were disturbed by the maid's sudden reappearance, saying said Mrs Markham would see her now.

She followed the servitor into a large, airy drawing room. Here again she was stunned by the size and opulence of the chamber. Sitting on a chaise-longue, Mrs Markham stood up as she entered. She smiled. "Ah, Dolly Deans."

At this Dolly curtsied. Edith Markham laughed. "No need to curtsey, Miss Deans. I am not the queen." Then after a couple of seconds her smiled widened. "Although some say I act like I am. I know they call me 'The Duchess' behind my back. Is that not so?" Dolly blushed and stammered. "I…I…I don't really…."

Mrs Markham laughed even more heartily. "It's all right, child, I know they do. I may be getting older, but I'm not deaf. And besides, 'The Duchess' isn't a bad name. There are worse names I could be called."

She indicated to Dolly to join her. "Here, bring your samples over here and we'll go through them together. I shall look to you for advice."

Sitting on the chaise longue together Dolly opened the case and they began to pore over the various materials. Soon the two were engaged in deep conversations about which colours and materials went best together. Dolly was flattered that so grand a lady took her opinions seriously and at times deferred to her suggestions.

The chime of a carriage clock caused Dolly to look at the time. She was surprised to see it was half past three. It was amazing that she and Mrs Markham had been chatting so long. Not only did she find the older woman gracious and charming but very open to listening to her ideas.

Finally Mrs Markham sat back. "Well, that was most interesting and helpful, Miss Deans. You are a bright young woman." At this Dolly felt her cheeks crimson. "Thank you, Mrs Markham." Closing the sample case she made ready to go.

"When you have made your final decision, ma'am, I'm sure we at Wentlock's will help in any way we can." As she said this Dolly stood up, ready to leave. Edith Markham looked at her quizzically. "Where are you going, child?" "Back to the shop, ma'am. If you do not need me for anything else."

Mrs smiled. "But we have not had tea yet. " Dolly looked puzzled. "Tea, Mrs Markham?" Edith Markham pointed to a chair. "Of course," she said, ringing a little porcelain bell, "we've been very busy and now it's time for tea."

As Dolly sat down the door opened and the maid entered pushing a little tea-trolley. Her eyes widened as she saw the plates of elegantly cut sandwiches, and scones filled with cream and jam. The teapot, cups, plates and saucers were of Willow pattern.

Handing her a napkin Mrs Markham lifted the tea-pot. "Now, shall I be mother?" They both laughed. The repast looked delicious and Dolly tried not to appear too greedy, nibbling delicately at the edge of her sandwich in what she hoped was a genteel manner. Her hostess looked at her. "Come now, Dolly Deans, those sandwiches are there to be eaten, not played with. You tuck in. I want those plates cleared."

Dolly did not need any encouragement and after that made hearty inroads into the food. As they ate they chatted. Dolly found Mrs Markham easy to talk to and before she realised it she had told her about her family and her father's death. Edith Markham shook her head in sympathy as heard this part of Dolly's story. But the older woman was also very interested in her young guest's other background, particularly her hopes of being a teacher, ending with the death of her father.

Finally tea was over. Dolly had never felt so deliciously full. She didn't think she would need to eat for a week after scoffing a half a dozen sandwiches, two scones and a piece of sponge cake. Mrs Markham seemed to take delight in her hearty appetite.

Packing away the sample case she thanked her hostess profusely. Mrs Markham waved away her expressions of gratitude. "Nonsense, child, it was a pleasurable afternoon which I enjoyed very much." She looked at the notes she had taken during the chat about the refurnishing. "I shall contact Wentlock's before I leave."

Dolly looked at her questioningly. "You are leaving, ma'am?" Mrs Markham nodded. "I am going to Italy for a month or two. My doctor recommends sunshine and sea air, so I have rented a villa on the shores of the Adriatic. Regain my health and strength."

"I wish you all good luck ma'am and hope you come back strong and well" Dolly said, sincerely. Edith Markham bowed her head in a graceful gesture of acknowledgement. "Thank you, Miss Deans. I appreciate your best wishes." She looked hard at Dolly for a few seconds. "You are an exceptional young woman and I see you going on to better things. When I return we must see what can be done for you."

As Dolly made her way back to the shop her mind raced with what had happened. Not only had Mrs Markham treated her with great kindness and respect, but had also suggested she had some idea to help her. She thought what a lovely day. Thomas and she were together again and there was some hint that her future might be exciting.

Arriving back at Wentlock's she hurriedly replaced all the samples before Miss Meredith swooped. Finally, having put everything away, she put on her pinafore and stood behind her counter. Her body was in the shop, but her mind was already floating into next Saturday, Thomas and the music hall.

Chapter Seven

The week had been endless. It seemed to Dolly that with every day that passed Saturday seemed to get further away rather than nearer. But now, here it was at last. She was waiting by the steps in front of her house, wearing her best dress, the one she had worn when she and Millie met Thomas in Victoria Park. Looking down she smiled as she saw Old Peggy's dog snoring gently. The late summer heat had made him drowsy. She was a little early but didn't want to spoil the start of the evening by keeping Thomas waiting, especially as this was to be their first proper outing as sweethearts.

Suddenly he appeared. He looked dashing and handsome in a dark brown suit and waistcoat.

She saw his hair had been trimmed. "Hello, Dolly Deans, hope I'm not late."

She laughed. "No, just got here myself." He took both her hands and stepped back in admiration. "You look lovely. Like a lady on a playbill in the theatre." Dolly curtsied in acknowledgement. "Why thank you kind sir."

Slipping her arm in his they began to walk along Whitechapel High Street. They spoke about their day and Thomas made her laugh when he told her he had to rescue a lady who had climbed up a tree to rescue her cat. The cat came down safely but the lady was stuck.

Leaving Whitechapel they walked along Mile End Road until they reached The Paragon Music Hall. Here, crowds milled around.

Vendors sold hot chestnuts, peanuts and fruit. One man, selling peaches, walked towards them, stopped and stared in shock for a couple of seconds, then suddenly turned and disappeared into the crowd. Doll y looked at Thomas. "What a strange thing." The young policeman laughed "Not really, I arrested him last week."

Approaching the entrance Dolly suddenly saw a familiar face. Millie was there bawling her wares. As well as a tray she had a large box, with a handle, at her feet, obviously carrying extra stock. The young vendor's eyes lit up. "Dolly! And Constable Turner. If I didn't know better I would say you two are walking out together now," she said with an arch lift of her eyebrow.

"You seem to be doing all right for yourself, Millie Ryan." Her friend shrugged modestly. "Pretty well, even if I do say so myself." She nudged the box with her toe. "Extra cakes. I sell out too quickly. If it goes on like this I'll need that market stall sooner than I thought, Dolly."

After Dolly arranged to meet her friend the next day, she and Thomas stepped into the foyer. Here, they approached the box-office where Thomas, bought for two tickets for the balcony. As these were the best and most expensive seats in the house, Dolly urged him not to be so generous, saying the gallery would do.

He waved away her protests. "Nothing too good for my girl," he said with a wink. The gallery seats were laid out as little private boxes, with red velvet chairs, trimmed with gold paint. Sitting down they had a wonderful view of the stage. Thomas turned to her. "Is this alright, my dear?" Dolly felt a glow of happiness. "It's lovely, Thomas. I feel like a queen." He squeezed her hand. "That's cause you are."

The orchestra in the pit struck up a lively opening number and the house lights went down. The music hall bill was packed with a variety of acts. Jugglers, comics, acrobats, singers and dancers. The audience were very enthusiastic and joined in all the popular songs of the day. Dolly and Thomas sang along with the rest. She had to smile at his rather tone deaf efforts. He was a terrible singer.

At around ten o'clock the evening ended with God Save the Queen. Thomas and Dolly made their way out with the rest of the audience. It had had a long time since she had felt so happy. Arm in arm the young couple strolled along the road to Whitechapel, talking about the show and laughing as they recalled the jokes the comics told.

However, as they nearer Whitechapel train station, they saw crowds milling around the entrance. People were frantically buying newspapers from the sellers who bawled out at the top of their voices that war had been declared. Easing their way to the front they could see the placards announcing war in South Africa.

Dolly felt a pang of apprehension. It had been such a perfect evening and the news of the conflict spoiled things. Thomas bought a paper and they both read anxiously. "Well, that's it. The balloon's gone up. There's an army going to fight the Boers," he said.

Strolling back to her house they stopped by the stairs. Dolly noticed there was no sign of the little dog. He had gone home for the night. They looked at each other and then Thomas placed is hand on her shoulders, leaned forward and kissed her gently. Dolly felt her heart race. It was her first proper kiss.

"Thank you for a lovely evening, Thomas," she said softly. He smiled. "Thank you for being with me. I felt so proud." They hugged and then

Dolly stepped back. "I'd better get in, mum will worry." He nodded. "As soon as I know my shift duty we'll go out again, shall we?" "Of course," she said smiling. He watched to make sure she was safely inside before walking away.

In the house she found her mother asleep by the fire. Dolly shook her by the shoulder gently. Mrs Deans looked up. "You're home, love. Did you have a nice time?" Dolly looked at her and smiled. "Yes, mum I had the most wonderful time in the world.

Chapter Eight

As they prepared the shop for opening that Monday morning all the staff could talk about was the approaching war. It seemed everyone was an expert on what was to come. There were many different opinions, but all seemed to agree that it would be over quickly. Even Miss Meredith thawed enough to venture a view, before clapping her hands together and ordering assistants to take their positions. She spoke especially caustically to Dolly. The spiteful manageress had not forgotten being snubbed by Mrs Markham.

The morning started unusually slowly. Dolly wondered if the sobering advent of war had put people off shopping. Her mind turned again to

Saturday night. It now all seemed like a dream. Thomas, so handsome and upright in his suit, the colour and gaiety of the music hall, the walk home and their first kiss.

"Deans! A word if you please!" Dolly was so lost in her musings that she didn't see the manageress until she stood glaring in front of her. "Yes, Miss Meredith," a nonplussed Dolly managed to mumble. "You are to report to Mr Wentlock, immediately!" barked Meredith.

Dolly felt a wave of trepidation sweep over her. Mr Wentlock! The head of the family business. She had only seen him a few times since starting. He was a severe-looking man who swept in occasionally, never usually giving the staff so much as a glance. Now he wanted to see her.

As she followed Miss Meredith upstairs and along a panelled corridor Dolly prepared herself for the worst. If she was to be dismissed she had no doubt the manageress was behind it. Meredith knocked at a polished door at the end of the corridor. A muffled voice bid them enter.

Walking in Dolly could see the shop owner sitting behind a massive oak desk. He looked up. "Ah, Miss Meredith. This is the girl?" He had a sharp, no-nonsense voice. The manageress smiled ingratiatingly. "Yes, Mr Wentlock. This is Miss Deans." Wentlock nodded. "Very well, that will be all, thank you."

Meredith smirked. "I will be happy to stay, if you need any extra information on her, Mr Wentlock." The man waved her offer with barely contained impatience. "No, that will be all." Giving a Dolly a side-long glance of resentment, the manageress sidled from the room. Dolly Deans stood uncertainly as Wentlock perused a letter in front of him. Finally he looked up and indicated she sit down

Dolly did so, perching nervously on the edge of the seat Finally he looked up. "I have received a letter concerning you, Miss Deans," he said, leaning back in the padded leather chair. "A letter, sir?" Dolly asked in a small voice.

"You know, Mrs Markham, of course." She nodded. "Yes sir." "Well, she has a written me a letter about you.. This letter" he said, holding up some sheets of paper. "A letter about me, sir?" Dolly mumbled. Wentlock ignored her question.

97

"It seems you were sent to help her with some refurbishment materials and advice." He leaned forward with a severe expression on his face. "Is that not so?" She felt herself tremble. "I did help the lady, sir. I did try my best."

The man held up a reassuring hand. "There is no need to look so worried, Miss Deans. Your best was more than good enough." He held up the letter again. "In this letter Mrs Markham sings your praises. Commends your manner and your skill. Says you are a credit to Wentlock's and only wishes to deal with you in future."

Dolly was stunned. She sat still, not quite knowing what to say. "I can't say how delighted I am," Wentlock said, putting down the letter. She was amazed to see his face crease in a smile.

"Not only has your conduct reflected very well on the shop, with a very old and valued customer, but it resulted in her making substantial purchases to the tune of several hundred pounds."

She felt a surge of relief. At least she would not be losing her position. "I was glad to be of service, sir." Mr Wentlock nodded approvingly and then checked another sheet of paper. "I see you are a junior assistant on a wage of fifteen shillings a week. Is that correct?" "Yes, sir."

Wentlock eyed her carefully for a few seconds. "Well, Miss Deans, such sterling work should be rewarded." He leaned his elbows on the desk. "What I propose is that you are given a raise to twenty two shillings and sixpence a week."

Dolly could not believe her ears. Twenty two shillings and sixpence! A fortune. She mumbled her thanks. Wentlock went on. "And, as you have shown aptitude and skill in advising customers, I am transferring you to Fine Furnishings where your talent can be used to greater effect."

He then adopted a brisker manner. "That will be arranged immediately. I will tell Miss Meredith that from tomorrow you will no longer be under her supervision." A great wave of joy and relief swept through Dolly. Not only were her wages being raised but she would be out from under the tyrannical Miss Meredith.

Leaving the room, after thanking Mr Wentlock profusely, Dolly felt she was floating on air.   The rest of the afternoon went past in a trance. With very little customers she was able to bask in her change of fortune. The extra money would make such a difference to the family.

As the shop closed up Meredith passed her and scowled. The manageress had obviously been informed of hers promotion. It was especially pleasurable for Dolly to wish her a cheerful goodnight. It would be the last one under her spitefulness.

The journey home seemed interminable. She was sure the tram driver was going slowly deliberately. Dolly could hardly wait to tell the family the good news. Almost running along the High Street she turned into her own street at a fast pace. Old Peggy's Dog looked at her expectantly. She pulled a rueful face. "Sorry, bow-wow, nothing for you now. But I'll bring something later."

Dolly burst into the room. "Mum, wonderful news." A worried-looking Billy jumped up from the table. "Thank heaven you're home, sis. Mum's poorly." Dolly ran over to her mother who was slumped before the fire. She looked anxiously at her. The older woman was pale. Her breath came in short gasps.

"Mum, what's wrong?" Mrs Deans smiled weakly. "Just a little turn, Dolly, nothing to worry about." Dolly felt her hands. They were cold. "I'll get a doctor, mum." Her mother shook her head. "We can't afford a doctor, love.

They would charge five shillings at least." Billy chimed in. "What about the doctor at the Sixpenny Dispensary?" Dolly patted him on the shoulder. "Good idea, Billy." She turned to her mother. "Do you think you could make it down there if we take it slowly, mum?"

Her mother nodded agreement. With Billy one side and Dolly on the other, and Liza holding her sister's skirt, they made their way to the Sixpenny Dispensary. Here, the poor of Whitechapel got the only health care they could afford.

An hour later, after waiting in a crowded surgery, they saw the sixpenny doctor, who diagnosed anaemia. He gave them a bottle of iron tonic and advised better eating, particularly beef and liver. The Deans, including mother, laughed at the thought.

After getting Mrs Deans home and giving her a hefty dose of the iron tonic, they put her to bed. About an hour or so later, her colour returned and she seemed to have fully recovered.

It was then Dolly told them the good news. The whole family were ecstatic. As she went to bed that night she thought of Thomas and her new job. It seemed that at last fortune was favouring the Deans.

Chapter Nine

Dolly finished carefully putting away a new delivery of tablecloths. Particular care was needed as they were a special order of Valenciennes lace. Very expensive. She looked around the Fine Furnishing department with a sigh of contentment. It was sedate and pleasant. None of the scurry and bustle of her previous position. But most of all she was free of the oppressive Miss Meredith.

In the five months since her transfer Dolly had thrived. She had a talent for décor and a pleasant manner with the customers. Miss Andrews, her supervisor, was a very different kettle of fish to Meredith. Kind and encouraging she engendered an atmosphere of calm and refinement in the department.

Life had also become easier in the Deans household. Dolly's raise in salary had made all the difference. They were able to buy meat and fresh vegetables once or twice a week. This had led to a significant improvement in her mother's health. Billy was still only getting casual work, but was trying hard for an apprenticeship.

Smiling she thought that even Old Peggy's Dog had benefited from her change of fortune as she was able to give the little mongrel more treats. She checked the clock. It was almost closing time. A thrill of anticipation ran through her. She was meeting Thomas later. It wasn't always easy as she worked longs hours in the shop and he often did shifts at all times of the day and night.

Despite this, in the months they had been walking out, they had fallen deeply in love. It was so obvious to everyone that Millie had already asked if she could make the wedding cake.

As she left the shop she saw Miss Meredith, scowling as usual. The other girls still in her department looked miserable Dolly's heart went out to them. Hurrying she managed to jump on the tram just as it was pulling away. On the conveyance all the talk was of the war in South Africa. It was now being called The Boer War. Reports of battles filled the front pages of the newspapers. Casualties were high on both sides.

The war stories always upset Dolly and she just wished it would end. As the tram trundled into Whitechapel High Street she remembered she had promised she would call in and see Millie on her way home. Her friend said she has something special to show her, but would not say what.

Intrigued Dolly hurried to the Ryan house. She knocked on the door which was thrown immediately open by a beaming Millie. "Dolly Deans, welcome to the baking empire of Miss Millie Ryan." Dolly laughed. "What are you on about, Mill?" Her friend, instead of inviting her inside, stepped onto the landing and beckoned her with a crook of her finger. Dolly giggled at her exaggeratedly mysterious manner. Going across the landing to the room opposite Millie took out a key and then pushed the door open.

As they stepped inside Dolly looked around in amazement. There were pots and pans, jugs and ladles and a dozen other baking implements all piled on a large table. In one corner were bags of flower. "What is this, Millie Ryan?" she said turning to her friend.

Millie smiled. "This is my bakery." "Your bakery?" Dolly asked quizzically. Bowing gracefully, Millie repeated, "My bakery." With an expansive sweep of her hands she proudly displayed her handiwork. "The cakes were selling like hot cakes, if you'll pardon the pun," she said with a grin. "My mum's kitchen was too small. Not enough room. So I rented this from the landlord. I can make double the cakes now."

Dolly shook her head in disbelief. "Millie, this is wonderful, I can't believe you've come so far so quickly. I'm so proud of you."

Millie nodded modestly at the compliment. "And that's not all. I heard an old lady at the market was giving up her pitch, so I bought her stall.!" Dolly was lost in admiration at her friend's entrepreneurial spirt. "All this in six months. Millie, you're a marvel."

The friends hugged on the landing and then Dolly hurried home to get ready to meet Thomas. At the stairs, waiting as usual, was Old Peggy's Dog. He sat up as he saw her coming, tail wagging in expectation. Dolly patted his head. "I'm spoiling you, you greedy little bow-wow." From her bag she took out the remnants of a meat pie she hadn't finished at lunch-time. "Here you are then." She grinned as the little canine wolfed it down.

"Now, Old Peggy's Dog. I have to run. I'm meeting someone very special." Racing into the house she ate a quick meal of bread and cheese, with Liza on her knee. Then, hugging the little girl, she said, "Liza, look what I got for you." From her bag she took out a little monkey on a string, suspended between two upright sticks. When the sticks were squeezed together the monkey did acrobatics. Liza squealed with delight.

Mrs Deans shook her head. "Dolly, you shouldn't out to have wasted your money on nonsense like that." "Oh, mum, it was only a few pennies. She doesn't have many toys."

Dolly ran into the other room and changed her blouse. Then, with a quick check of her hair, she was out the door in a flash. Thomas and she had agreed to meet at a tea-room near the London Hospital as he would just be coming off duty in that vicinity. Her heart beat with excitement, it always did when she was meeting Thomas. She was head over heels in love with him.

The early winter night had set in and the streets of Whitechapel were dotted with the first coatings of frost. The cold had turned people's breath smoky on the air. Dolly arrived at the tea shop. She could see Thomas was already in there, still in his uniform. Waving cheerily to him through the window she noticed his smile didn't seem as wide and welcoming as usual.

Inside, the tea-room was cosy and comfy. The place smelled of warm scones and toast. Kitty rushed over to Thomas and kissed him lightly on the cheek before sitting down. "I'm not late am I?" she asked. Thomas shook his head. "No, I've just got here." Looking at the menu he asked, "What would you like? A scone? A sandwich?" Dolly shrugged. "A scone and tea would be fine." The tea-room was packed and it took him a little time to attract a waitress. When the servitor arrived he ordered tea for two, but just one scone for Dolly.

She was surprised. Usually he had a very healthy appetite and seldom passed up the chance to eat. Looking at him with concern she said, "Aren't you hungry, Thomas?" He shook his head. "No, no, I had something earlier." There was something in his demeanour that wasn't right in Dolly's eyes. Thomas always an open and easy nature. Now he seemed tense and uneasy.

Instead of launching into his usual cheery chatter Thomas was somewhat monosyllabic. Answering her questions tersely. Dolly tried to lift the mood by telling him funny stories about her customers that day. He responded with a weak attempt at smiling.

After the tea and scone arrived they sat in silence for a few seconds, Thomas stirring his tea continuously. Finally Dolly could stand it no longer.

"Thomas, what's wrong?" The young policeman tried to act surprised. "Wrong? There's nothing wrong." She leaned forward. "I know you Thomas Turner, I know you better than I know myself. Now there's something wrong, so tell me what?"

He sat in silence. Dolly felt herself grow fearful as she contemplated the worst. Finally she spoke. "Do you wish to end this? Have you found another, is that it?" Thomas looked at her, his eyes wide with amazement . "Another?

Oh, no, Dolly, I love you more than my life, I swear." "Then tell me what's wrong."

The young policeman took a deep breath. "I've enlisted." Dolly's brow furrowed in puzzlement "Enlisted? What do you mean?" He took a sip of tea. "In the army. I've enlisted to go and fight in South Africa."

A chill feeling swept over her heart and for a few moments she could not speak. When she did her voice seemed to come from far away. "The army? You've joined the army? How could you do this, Thomas? How could you do this to me, to *us*?"

"It's my duty. To serve my country." he blurted out defiantly. Dolly felt as if she had stepped into a nightmare. "Your duty? You do your duty

116

already, as a policeman." Thomas shook his head. "It's not the same, Dolly. Fighting for your country is different."

They sat in a little tableau of misery. Each lost in the immensity of the matter that had just passed between them. Dolly fought back the tears. He put his hand over hers. "Dolly," he said tenderly, "it's something I felt I needed to do. Me and lots of the other constables at the hostel. We're all going together. Look after each other so to speak."

Dolly Deans took out a handkerchief and dabbed at her eyes. She kept her head bowed low. Finally Thomas broke the silence in a tone of forced cheeriness. "We've all been told our jobs are safe. When we get back we can step right back   into the police, just where we left off."

Dolly rose slowly from the table. Thomas looked at her. "Where are you going?" Shaking her head she said "Home, I need to go home, Thomas." He stood up. "Hold on I'm coming with you." He threw a few coins on the table and then took her arm.

Outside the cold had become more intense. Dolly shivered but she wasn't sure if it was the weather or what had just happened. Thomas took her arm and slipped it through his. They began to walk back towards Whitechapel, none of them speaking.

Finally Dolly stopped, buried her face into his chest and shook with silent sobs. People passing stared at the unusual sight of a policeman holding a crying woman. When she had regained her composure they made their way to way to her house. Standing there Thomas tried be optimistic. "You know it will be over by Christmas. Probably find it's all done by the time we've done our training. That takes about twelve weeks. We probably won't even leave the barracks." "Goodnight, Thomas," Dolly said sadly.

He turned and walked away slowly. Dolly stood there until he was gone. She felt her heart would break. The thought of going into the house yet was unbearable. She needed someone to talk to that wasn't family.

Retracing her steps she made her way to Millie's house. After her friend opened the door and took one look at her tearful face she led her across to her bakery. Here she put on the kettle , made them both a cup of tea and listened in amazement as Dolly told her story. When she had finished Millie whistled silently.

"Well there's a find how-do-you-do. That's the last thing I would have expected. Thomas Turner, first a policeman, now a soldier-boy. One good thing thought, Dolly, you have to admit he looks handsome in a uniform."

Despite herself Dolly laughed. Taking a sip of tea she looked at her friend. "What am I going to do, Millie?" Her friend pulled a wry face. "Not much you can do now, Dolly. What's done is done. What matters now is how you want to handle this?"

"Handle it?" Dolly asked. Millie poured another cup of mahogany-brown tea. "Yes, do you want to wait for him or not?" Dolly's eyes flared in indignation. "Of course I want to wait for him, Millie, I love him." Her friend patted her gently on the shoulder. "Then you already know what to do. Just let him know you'll be waiting."

Chapter Ten

Dolly held Thomas' hand tightly as they made their way into Liverpool Street Station. They stepped carefully as the ice had made the pavements treacherous. Despite looking forward to their little adventure, inside she felt a deep sadness. This Sunday was the last before he left for his army training.

Thomas had suggested a rail trip out to Chingford, a little village on the edge of Epping Forest. When they were children they, and thousands of other people of the east end, would make this journey in the summer. To roam the forest and enjoy the massive fair which was held once a year.

After buying the tickets they made their way on to the great steam train which hissed impatiently, waiting to go. As the day was so bitter there were not many passengers so they had a carriage to themselves.

"Are you too cold?" Thomas asked solicitously. "I can adjust the heat." Dolly shook her head. "I'm fine. " The last weeks had been hard on both of them and now, as the their last few hours together dwindled down, they were both determined to make their last day a happy one.

"Do you remember when we all used to come out here in the summer?" Dolly said, squeezing his hand. "I remember eating so many toffee apples I was sick on the way home." They both laughed and then he kissed her gently. The suddenly blast of a guard's whistle signalled the off. With a great hiss of steam and a juddering of the carriages the train pulled out of the station.

Dolly was amazed that in such a short time the scenery changed from the grim houses of the east end to trees and fields. Holding hands they stared at the passing countryside. Deeply in love and dreading their parting.

In a less than an hour they pulled into Chingford Station. As they stepped outside, the icy air caught the backs of their throats. It seemed so much colder away from the city.

"Shall we find somewhere to eat? " Thomas suggested. Dolly shook her head. "No, let's walk in the forest first. It looks lovely." They began to stroll through the greenery. The frost-dappled trees and grass made it look like a Christmas card scene.

As they walked they rarely spoke, each lost in their thoughts. Coming to Connaught Water, a large lake in the forest, they tried skimming stones. Much to Thomas' chagrin Dolly was much better at this and won every time.

By now they were both feeling hungry and were glad when they arrived at Butler's Retreat, a little eating place opened especially for visitors to the forest. Stepping inside they both enjoyed the wave of hot air which enveloped them. A waitress led them to a table. After a look at the menu they ordered thick vegetable broth, with slices of bread and butter. It was ideal for a bitterly cold day.

Warmed by the broth their talk grew more cheerful. Thomas was even more sure the war would not last much beyond Christmas. His confident tone reassured Dolly and by the time their order of tea and scones had arrived both were in a jollier mood.

"You know, Dolly," Thomas said, taking a hanky and wiping a blob of jam from the corner of her mouth, "during the training we get leave, so we'll still see each other lots. And then, as I said before, it'll probably be over before I get to know one end of a rifle from another."

Dolly laughed. She wanted to believe he was right. When they finished she looked out the window. It was growing dark already. She drained the last dregs of her tea. "I suppose we should get back. I don't like to leave mum alone too long. She hasn't been well."

As she began to rise Thomas held her arm. "Just a minute, Dolly, there's something I want to ask you." She smiled uncertainly as his face suddenly took on a serious expression. "What is it, Thomas? Is there something wrong?" He took a small ball of tissue paper from his waistcoat pocket and unwrapped it, revealing a beautiful engagement ring. "It was my gran's. Mum kept it for me until I found the girl I wanted. I've found her."

Chapter Eleven

"Well done, Miss Deans. That idea you had for the window display showed imagination. Keep up the good work." Dolly blushed slightly at Miss Andrews compliment. "Thank you, Miss Andrews" Her manageress smiled and walked away. Since moving to Fine Furnishings Dolly found she had an eye for colour and design. More and more she was involved in presentation as well as sales.

Although the hours were still as long at least she found some satisfaction in the tasks. Since Thomas had left four weeks ago she had tried to bury the heartache by keeping herself busy. When not at the shop she would help at home and often visited Millie.

Her friend's business was thriving. Shortly after setting up the stall she was already talking about a shop. Dolly always knew Millie would make something of herself. Even when they were children she was full of energy and drive. Always suggesting imaginative schemes.

Thomas had already written to her several times telling her about the training and the chaps he was with. He made it sound jolly, all a bit of a wheeze, but Dolly now read the newspapers avidly and knew the terrible toll of lives the war was taking.

She looked at the clock. An hour to closing time. After work she would have a meal with the family. Then go to Castle Alley baths for a long hot soak. Later she was meeting Millie. As she made her way across the shop floor she suddenly saw a familiar figure talking to Miss Andrews. It was Mrs Markham. She looked well and still had the remnants of healthy tan from her months in Italy.

Dolly caught her eye and waved. In response Edith Markham indicated she wait. After finishing her talk with Miss Andrews she walked over. "Miss Deans, how lovely to see you. I've often thought about you and wondered how you were doing."

Dolly had to resist the impulse to curtsy. "I'm doing very well, ma'am. Thanks to you."

"Thanks to me?" "Yes, ma'am, the letter you wrote to Mr Wentlock, it had me promoted and given a much nicer job. Thank you again."

Mrs Markham waved away her thanks. "It was nothing, child, I only told the truth. But I am glad they have recognised your talents." Dolly said "You're looking very well, ma'am. The stay in Italy has done you good." The older woman shook her head. "Perhaps, I will never be fighting fit, but, as far as it goes, I am well. And your family, Miss Deans, they are well?"

Dolly could see the other assistants looking at them curiously. A mere server chatting with one of the shop's wealthiest customers. She turned her attention to Mrs Markham. "Yes, ma'am, quite well. My mother is poorly at times but on the whole all is well."

Markham looked at her smiled. "And is there a young man in your life?" The younger woman coloured. " A young man, ma'am?" Edith Markham laughed softly. Dolly thought it made her look and sound like a girl. "Yes, a young man, is that so unlikely for such a pretty girl?"

Holding out her finger Dolly showed the engagement ring sparkling on her finger. Mrs Markham beamed. "How lovely. And your young man, what does he do?" "He's a policeman ma'am, but he's just joined the army."

A frown crossed the older woman's face. "Yes, this wretched war. Such a waste. Such a waste." She took out a little pocket watch. "Well, I must be going. It was nice to see you again, Miss Deans." Dolly smiled "And you, ma'am."

As she turned to go Mrs Markham stopped. "If you ever decide that you would like to leave shop work, Dolly Deans, come and see me. I think we might find you something more interesting."

As Mrs Markham approached the exit, one of the other assistant rushed to open the door. For the rest of the hour Dolly wondered what her last remarks had meant. Finally the clock chimed six and the staff hurried from the shop. A couple of the girls lived in the east end so they and Dolly travelled together chatting about their day. But just before alighting one of them said her uncle had just been killed in South Africa.

This resurrected all Dolly's fears and it was in low spirits she arrived at her building. Sitting there, as usual, was Old Peggy's Dog. He showed his new trick. He raised his paw. Dolly couldn't help grinning. " You old rascal, you know that makes you look adorable, don't you?" She patted his head and then took out a piece of paper, holding a sausage. "Here you are, you've earned it, you crafty old thing."

The sausage was gone in a flash. Dolly walked up the stairs and into their rooms. On the sideboard was a letter. She recognised the handwriting immediately. It was from Thomas.

Excitedly she tore it open and began to read. Billy teased her,. "What's he saying, sis, lots of kissy kissy-kissy?" As he said this he made exaggerated kissing noises. Liza laughed delightedly and copied the noises as best she could.

Dolly shot her brother a warning glance. "You be quiet, Billy Deans." Mrs Deans pointed a finger at him. "Don't be horrible. Billy. How would you like it if your sweetheart was far away?"

Billy pulled a face. "A sweetheart? Me? Groooo." Again Liza ran about making the sound. Dolly let out a squeal of delight. "He's getting leave, mum. In a week or two." Her mother clapped her hand together. "That's lovely, dear. Now let's eat."

After a meal of sliced ham and potatoes, which Dolly hardly noticed as her head was full of Thomas coming home, she hurried out to the baths. Later she made her way to a tea-room in Mile End to meet Millie.

Her friend was there already and had ordered tea and cakes. Dolly smiled as her friend eyed the bakes with professional distain. " Who made these cakes? Old Mother Hubbard?" They both laughed. Soon they were swapping stories about their daily lives. Millie was delighted to hear Thomas was coming home.

"You know, Dolly, we never had a proper celebration of your engagement." "Yes, I know, but the way things are. You know. Anyway, your stall's going from strength to strength."

Millie winked. "More than you think, girl?" Dolly looked at her curiously. "What's that supposed to mean, Millie Ryan?" Her friend said, " Well, a lady who runs a bakery is closing it down. Her husband is ill and they're moving to the coast. There's a year left on the lease. She came to my stall and asked if I wanted the last year very cheap."

Dolly stared in amazement. "And what did you say?" Mille grinned. "I took it of course. You gotta take a chance, girl." "You, with a shop, already? Millie, you are amazing," Dolly gasped.

The rest of the hour was spent excitedly discussing Millie's great plan. Eventually they parted outside the tea-room, Dolly was delighted at her friend's news. But now all her thoughts were centred on Thomas's return.

Chapter Twelve

Time seemed to stand still for Dolly. Thomas had written to say he would be home for the weekend. Now, it was Thursday and her impatience was almost unbearable. One thing which made the waiting easier was her work at Wentlock's. Miss Andrews was placing more and more trust in her.

She was meeting her manageress in a few minutes to discuss the shop's plans for Christmas. It was an important time for Wentlock's and they put great store by their display. While she waited she contemplated buying a new dress for Thomas's home-coming.

Dolly had seen a lovely red velvet dress in one of the shops in Aldgate and thought it would be perfect. The expense worried her. But she was making more money and had managed to save a little.

Still, could she justify such self-indulgence? On the other hand, Dolly thought, she had not had a new dress for more than a year. Almost all her raise in wages had gone into making life easier at home for the family. Surely she deserved just this one thing for herself? The clincher in her internal debate was how she would look in the dress when she met Thomas. She would buy it on the way home.

"You dreaming of Christmas already, Miss Deans?" She turned to see a smiling Miss Andrews by her side. "No, Miss Andrews." Clapping her hands together in a business-like manner the manageress said. "Now, Christmas displays and décor. Important decisions. And I'm relying on you to come up with some imaginative ideas, Miss Deans. So, is your thinking cap on?" Dolly nodded. "Yes, Miss Andrews."

Before long Dolly and Miss Andrews were deep in discussion about tinsel, holly wreaths, reindeer and sleighs. But every now and then in Dolly's mind floated the image of a red velvet dress.

When the day finally ended Dolly rushed for the tram, ignoring the other girls shouts to wait for them. Getting off the conveyance she hurriedly made her way down to Aldgate. A horrible feeling crossed her mind. What if it had been sold?

A wave of relief swept over her as she saw the dress was still in the window. It was even lovelier than she remembered. The deep red velvet material caught the light, making it almost shimmer. Dolly walked in to the shop. The assistant hurried over.

"Can I help you madam?" Pointing to the window Dolly said, "The red velvet dress, I'd like to try it on please." The assistant beamed. "A wonderful choice, madam. It would suit your colouring perfectly."

The dress was taken from the window and Dolly took it into a little cubicle. She put it on and stared at herself in the mirror. It was beautiful and fitted perfectly. She looked like a princess. Stepping outside she looked at the assistant. "What do you think?" The girl put her hands to her mouth. "Oh, madam, that dress is made for you. Absolutely made for you."

Dolly nodded decisively. "I'll take it please. Just one thing, I should like to place a deposit and pay for it when I collect it on Friday. Is that all right?" The assistant furrowed her brow. "Well, that is not normal practice. This dress could sell any time." Dolly felt her heart sink. She wanted the dress so badly.

But then the assistant's expression softened. "But, madam, as you and that dress are made for each other then we can accept a deposit.

However," she said warningly, "if it is not collected on Friday your deposit will be forfeit."

Dolly handed over a few coins and then left the shop. Relief and excitement flooded through her. Peering through the window she could see the assistant put the dress and a hanger. Her dress! A special dress. To wear for Thomas.

Chapter Thirteen

For a moment it didn't seem as if he was on the train. Dolly's heart pounded anxiously. Almost every passenger had gotten off. Suddenly she saw a figure step down from the end carriage. It was Thomas. He looker taller and straighter in his army uniform. She waved and they ran towards each other.

Thomas caught her up in his arms and whirled her around. Then they kissed. Dolly felt tears of happiness roll down her cheeks. He smiled. "Nice to see you, Dolly Deans." "Nice to see you, Thomas Turner." They laughed and then walked arm in arm out of the station.

Dolly was surprised at how soldierly he looked in so short a time. Ramrod straight, shoulders back. A long way from the mischievous boy she had grown up with. As they walked along he told her of the training. The gymnastics, the marching, the drills, the rifle practice. His tone made it seem like fun but Dolly knew the real purpose, Thomas was being prepared for war. But she drove these thoughts from her mind. He was home. They had Saturday night and all day Sunday together.

"Are you staying at the police hostel? she asked as they crossed Bishopsgate. Thomas shook his head. "No, officially I'm not in the police now. I'll stay with mum and dad." He kissed her lightly on the nose. "I'll go and change out of my uniform then we can go and have a nice dinner somewhere."

They walked arm in arm to Thomas' home, both lost in the happiness of being together. When they arrived to his surprise his parents were not in. A note on the table said they had to go at once to an address in Foster Street, it was very urgent that he and Dolly must come as soon as they could.

Both were mystified and worried. After he quickly changed into his civilian clothes they hurried to Foster Street. The address was a shop front. Dolly looked at Thomas. "Are you sure this is the right number? He took out the note his parents had left. "Yes, this is it." Dolly thought it seemed like a bad joke, but couldn't imagine Thomas's parents playing such a trick.

They approached the door. It wasn't locked. Pushing it open cautiously they stepped inside. Suddenly they were met by a blast of singing as a lively version of 'For He's a Jolly Good Fellow' struck up. Dolly could not believe her eyes. She and Thomas's family and friends were gathered. The shop was decorated with streamers and balloons. Tables were laid out with cakes and sandwiches. There were also pots of tea and a few bottles of beer for drinks.

Thomas and Dolly looked at each other in delighted surprise. Millie stepped forward and hugged Dolly. "You didn't think we were going to let you get engaged without a party, did you, Dolly Deans?" Dolly knew this must have been her friend's doing. No one else would have the imagination and energy arrange it.

147

"Thank you, Mill, thank you more than I can say." She kissed her friend on the cheek and whispered, "Is this going to be your shop?" Millie grinned. "The best cakes in Whitechapel by Christmas."

Millie then hugged Thomas before the young couple were surrounded by family and friends all offering congratulations. Baby Liza ran to Dolly with her arms raised, demanding to be lifted up. Dolly grabbed her and whirled her round, the little girl helpless with laughter as she got dizzy.

Mrs Deans came over. "I'm so happy, love," she said as she kissed her daughter. She then looked with mock severity at Thomas. "And you, Thomas Turner, you take good care of her or you'll answer to me." The young soldier smiled. "I'll guard her with my life, Mrs Deans."

In the corner Billy looked over and winked at Dolly as he crammed a cream cake, whole, into his mouth. Suddenly music was heard. Someone had brought a phonograph. These were expensive and few people in the east end could afford one. Dolly suspected this was Millie's doing again.

From the phonograph a tinny voice quavered out a version of 'The Man Who Broke the Bank at Monte Carlo' and people began to dance. When Dolly took off her coat there was a collective burst of oohs and aahs as they saw her dress. Compliments flowed. Thomas looked at her and said, "You look like a princess, Dolly. I'm the proudest man in London right now."

He bowed and offered his arm. They began to dance, looking into each others eyes. Dolly was touched by the efforts people had made on her behalf. Deep down she would have preferred if the evening had just been as they had originally planned. After waiting so long to see Thomas, a quiet dinner, with just the two of them, would have been heavenly.

Then she chided herself mentally for such a thought. Shame on you, Dolly Deans for being so ungracious, after the trouble people have gone to. She cheered herself up with the thought that she and Thomas would have the whole day together on Sunday.

The evening was huge success and about ten o 'clock things began to break up. The shop was littered with crockery and half-eaten crusts. Several people offered to help clear up. Millie would not hear of any of the Deans doing this, Dolly was the guest of honour.

Mrs Deans and her family made their way home, with Thomas carrying a sleeping Liza. At the house entrance Billy took his baby sister as he and his mother went indoors.

Dolly hugged Thomas tightly. "You have no idea how I've longed to do this, Thomas." He held her even closer. "And me, dear. How many nights I've lain awake in the barracks, thinking of you, picturing you, missing you."

They held each other in silence for a few seconds. Then Dolly looked into his eyes. "You will stay safe and come back to me, Thomas, promise?" He lifted her chin and kissed her softly on the lips. "Course I will Dolly Deans. Half a dozen armies couldn't keep me away from you."

They then heard the town hall clock strike eleven. "Better go. Getting late. But I'll see you tomorrow," Dolly said, taking his hand. "I'll come round bright and early. We can go into the west end. See how the toffs live. Have lunch somewhere posh." They kissed again. Thomas watched to make sure she got in safely before walking away.

As Dolly climbed the stairs, a thought went through her mind. That was the first time Thomas hadn't said the war would be over by Christmas.

Chapter Fourteen

Millie grinned as she saw a blob of paint on the point of Dolly's nose. The two friends had been working hard to get the shop ready to open before Christmas. Dolly was glad of the chance to keep busy. It was two weeks since Thomas had gone back to his barracks and she was heavy of heart. So, helping her friend was just what she needed to occupy her mind.

She had written and asked him if he would get leave at Christmas and was waiting for his answer. Almost as if she could read her mind, Millie called across. "Any word from Thomas, yet?" Dolly shook her head. "No, I only wrote three days ago," "No news is good news, that's what they say, "Millie replied, as she placed lining paper on a shelf.

Stepping back from the shelves the young baker   looked   around   the   shop   with   an expression   of   satisfaction.   The   place   was transformed.   In the last two weeks she and Dolly had scrubbed it clean, washed down the shelving,   laid   linoleum   and   polished   the windows. The baking trays gleamed and the new oven was ready.

"You know, Dolly, I think that's just about it." Her friend stood up. "Looks tickety-boo, Mill." Putting down her paint brush she walked over to Millie. "When do you reckon to open?" Millie Ryan put down the scissors. " The day after

tomorrow." Dolly's eyes widened in disbelief. "
The day after tomorrow? Are you sure?"

Millie walked around. "Place is ready, I'm
ready, Christmas is just over two weeks away.
People will want to buy mince pieces,
gingerbread, Twelfth cake. No time to waste."
Dolly was constantly in awe of her friend's
boldness. Millie Ryan feared nothing and that
was why she would succeed.

"So, what say you we go for a nice plate of pie
and mash.? My treat." Dolly laughed. "You're
on, Miss Ryan, but I must warn you I'm
starving so bring plenty of money.

The friends put on their coats and made for
the door. Here, Millie stopped and looked at
Dolly with a foreboding expression. "There's

just one thing, Dolly, something I've got to tell you. Something serious."

Dolly felt butterflies in her stomach. Millie was never serious. "What is it, Mill?"

Her friend leaned forward in a confidential manner. "You've got a blob of white paint on your nose."

"Millie Ryan," "Dolly said, playfully pushing her friend, "you frightened the life out of me then." Laughingly they made their way to the café where, after a meal, Dolly set out for home. While she was with Millie her friend's high spirits kept worrying thoughts about Thomas being away, but now as she alone the doubts came flooding back.

As she climbed the stairs she hoped fervently that a letter was waiting. It would be wonderful if they could spend Christmas together. When she walked in her mother was sewing and Liza was playing with the little toy monkey Dolly had bought her.

"Hello mum, has there been any...?" Her mother smiled and held out a letter. "Just came an hour ago." Dolly rushed over and tore open the envelope. After a moment her face became a mask of dismay. Mrs Deans looked at her with concern. "What's the matter, love?"

Holding out the letter, with tears in her eyes, Dolly said, "He can't come home, mum. His regiment, they're being sent to South Africa before Christmas."

Chapter Fifteen

It was Christmas Eve and the last customers were just leaving Wentlock's. The two weeks leading up to the holiday had been frantic. To Dolly it was a blessing. It kept her mind occupied. The news from Thomas that he was going to South Africa had broken her heart.

The newspapers had been filled with stories about the war escalating. Instead of the short, sharp campaign so many had predicted it now seemed as it would be a long, protracted struggle. The thought of Thomas going into such danger was unbearable.

On the stroke of six the shop doors were locked. Dolly and the rest of the staff were able to catch their breaths. All that remained was to tidy up and place covers over the goods and display cases. They had been told Mr Wentlock had laid on a small Christmas buffet as thanks for all the efforts they had put in.

With the rest of the assistants they made their way to the staff canteen. One of the girls grumbled to Dolly that their working day was over and Mr Wentlock was thanking them in their own time.

In the canteen a spread of sandwiches, cakes and mince pies had been set out. The staff fell on them ravenously. It had been a long day and none of them had eaten for several hours. They chatted and swapped stories of awkward customers until one of the department heads, Mr

Etherington, clapped his hands together and asked for silence.

"Thank you ladies and gentlemen." Dolly and some of the other girls smiled at his manner. He was always very pompous. "Mr Wentlock would like to say a few words."

There was a smattering of applause. Wentlock smiled. "Thank you. Thank you. Now it's Christmas Eve and I know you are all anxious to get home to your families." Dolly smothered a grin as the girl beside her whispered "Yes we are, so get on with it, you old windbag."

The store owner went on. "You have all worked very hard this last month and as a token of my thanks I have arranged that you all have a bonus of five shillings in your next wage packets." This brought a round of applause. He held up his hands for silence. "I have just one more announcement to make. Sad to say, Miss Andrews, head of our Fine Furnishing Department will be leaving." Dolly felt dismayed. Miss Andrews was her mentor. She had given her a chance to develop her skills and talent.

"We will be sorry to lose her, but she is taking up a post at Harrods as head of their Fine Furnishings. Well done, Miss Andrews." He started another round of applause. When this died down he continued. "And taking her place as head of the department here will be Miss Merededith."

Chapter Sixteen

When she woke up on Christmas morning Dolly's yuletide spirit was rather muted. All night she had been plagued with worries about Thomas and also the dread of once more being under the baleful glare of Miss Meredith.

But she was determined not to allow her own despondency to spoil the holiday for the rest of the family. Over the past few months she had been secretly putting a few pennies away to make sure the Deans would celebrate Christmas properly.

Mrs Deans was already up and Liza was running around excitedly, sensing the day was special. Dolly handed them their presents. For her sister a spinning top, which caused the little girl to squeal with joy. She gave a Billy a penknife, something he had wanted for months. Her mother was delighted with a Paisley Pattern scarf.

In turn her mother gave her a blouse fashioned from the top half of her best silk dress. Dolly was especially touched as the dress was her mother's most treasured possession. It had been the last gift her husband had given her before he died.

Soon the smell of cooking filled the Deans home. Christmas dinner was to be boiled beef, roast potatoes, peas and carrots. Covered with thick gravy. For afters Mrs Deans made plum pudding with custard.

Billy drove his mother and sister mad asking every ten minutes when dinner would be ready. At last they all sat around the table, eyes gleaming at the feast. Mrs Deans had to stop her son gorging everything in sight. She tapped his fingers hard with a spoon.

"Billy Deans, if you grab like that one more time I'll chop your hands off."

There was laughter and joking and for a little while Dolly managed to forget her worries.

When the meal was over, Dolly washed up. She took the few scraps left over and put them on a piece of wax paper for Old Peggy's Dog. The afternoon grew dark and the family settled around the fire. Liza played with her top, while Billy took a piece of scrap wood and tried to carve a whistle. Mrs Dean looked replete and content by the fire.

Dolly put on her coat. "I'm going to see Millie, mum. Got a present for her." Her mother nodded, half dozing. "Alright, love. You be careful. With that frost the pavements are slippery."

Closing the door she slipped out. At the bottom of the stairs, as usual, was the little canine. He looked at her expectantly, tail wagging furiously. Putting the scraps in front of him she watched as he wolfed them down. Patting the dog on the head she said, "Merry Christmas Old Peggy's Dog. At least you don't have my worries, you lucky thing."

Dolly made her way along the High Street. Whitechapel was lively, despite the bitter cold and the thick coating of frost on the windows and pavements. Different coloured lights shone in the windows and she could hear singing from the public houses. She reached Millie's house and was welcomed in.

Like her own family, the Ryans had obviously eaten themselves to bursting point. Mr and Mrs Ryan lay slumped in armchairs each side of the fire. "Merry Christmas, Dolly," her friend said, giving her a hug. "And the same to you, Millie," Dolly replied. Turning to the couple each side of the fire she also wished them the season's greetings.

Dolly handed Millie a little package. On opening it her friend saw it was a lace handkerchief. "Oh, that is lovely, Dolly. Thank you ever so much. Wait a minute, I got something for you." She handed Dolly a box. "Don't open it till you get home. It's a gingerbread cake. Just right for a cup of tea at Christmas."

Millie put on her coat and they made their way back along the High Street. The air was bracing but cold. Both pulled their coats more tightly around them. They reached their old school. "You remember the first time we met, Millie? It was right by that door, our first day. We were in Miss Hamilton's class."

Millie Ryan smiled. "Lots of water gone under the bridge since then, Dolly. Look at us now.

You a fancy decorator for toffs…" Dolly cut in, "And you the best baker in Whitechapel." They laughed. Then Dolly told her about her worries with Thomas and having to face Miss Meredith again.

She shook her head helplessly. "I don't know what to do, Millie." Her friend put a comforting arm around her shoulder. " This is Whitechapel, Dolly. You do what Whitechapel people always do. Grin and bear it."

Chapter Seventeen

It had been a mixed Christmas for Dolly. Time with family had been happy, despite her worries about Thomas, but now she was once again under the thumb of the tyrannical Miss Meredith. As soon as she returned after the holiday it became apparent that Meredith would not give her any sort of tasks beyond serving and clearing up.

The manageress seemed to reserve the most tedious duties for Dolly. It was obvious she had not forgotten what she saw as a slight when her assistant was chosen over her by Mrs Markham.

The new century had just begun and Dolly Deans could not have felt any lower in spirits. Thomas sent her letters, jokey and full of encouragement. But she knew this was for her benefit and that the war was growing more intense.

With the support of the family and the cheerfulness of Millie she might have been able to cope with the heartache, but the daily harassment by Miss Meredith was impossible to bear. But Dolly had no option but to endure this, her family needed her wages. Then, just after New Year, as she sat in the small gardens having lunch, she suddenly remembered what Mrs Markham had once said. *If you ever decide you would like to leave shop work, Dolly Deans, come and see me.*

Hope sprung up in her breast. Mrs Markham would not have said this if she did not mean it.

She was not that the type of person, surely? Dolly felt a sense of relief. At least this offered some way out of her misery. She decided she would write that night. With this resolution in place she went back to work with a lighter heart.

After another afternoon of Miss Meredith's spite Dolly could hardly wait to get home. Her mother was visiting a neighbour and Billy had not come back yet. So, after a quick meal of bread and cheese, she sat down and composed a careful letter to Mrs Markham. As she did so Dolly took pains to write in her best copperplate handwriting. Miss Burgess had always told her that handwriting was the same as a first impression. It told of the character. When she was finished she was tempted to rush out and post the letter but then thought she could save

172

the price of a stamp and put it through the door before work.

With this completed she sat down to write a long letter to Thomas. She filled it with gossip about Whitechapel, about the family and Millie's shop. One thing she didn't mention was the war or what was happening to him. This was something she could not bear to think about.

Tidying up she waited until her mother came in before going to bed. Although she was very tired her mind raced with thoughts and worries about Thomas. It was a while before she fell asleep. And when she did she dreamt of holding a stack of boxes while a giant Miss Andrews piled more and more on top.

Chapter Eighteen

Dolly took a deep breath and knocked on the door. It had been three days since Mrs Markham had replied to her letter, inviting her to Sunday tea. After writing she had not heard back for nearly a week and had assumed the there was no position for her in the Markham household. Resigned to facing weeks , months or even years of Miss Meredith she was thrilled when a letter, with the Markham crest on the back of the envelope, arrived.

In it she apologised graciously for the delay, as she had been out of town for a while. Now, Dolly waited pounding heart to see what the meeting might bring. She was willing to do almost anything offered. Maid. Work in the kitchen. Even scrub the floors.

The door opened and the same servitor who had let her in on her first visit ushered her inside. Waiting in the grand hall she saw that it had been painted recently. After a minute the maid led her to the drawing room. Mrs Markham stood by the fireplace.

"Miss Deans, how lovely to see again," she said as she stepped forward to shake Dolly's hand. "Please sit down," The older woman sat opposite. Dolly could see she looked more fragile now that the last hint of her sun tan had faded. Smiling she asked "Are you well?" "Yes, ma'am. " Mrs Markham nodded. "Good. Good.

And your family?" "Very well, thank you, ma'am."

Edith Markham picked up the little porcelain bell and rang for tea. She leaned forward. "May I ask about your young man? He is safe and well I hope?" Dolly shrugged. "He is in South Africa, ma'am, but I have not heard any bad news, thank goodness."

The door opened and the maid appeared with the tea-trolley. It was again laden with sandwiches and scones. Dolly had told herself she would try not to scoff so much this time. But with the sight of the delicious food before her she immediately abandoned that resolve.

Mrs Markham pointed to the teapot. "Why don't you be mother this time?" They both laughed then Dolly carefully filled the cups. Edith Markham sat back.

"I read your letter with great interest. By the way, I must compliment you on your beautiful handwriting. A real pleasure to find such elegance and clarity." Dolly gave a nod of acknowledgment and silently thanked Miss Burgess.

"I take it you are no longer happy at Wentlock's?" Trying to think of a diplomatic answer Dolly shifted in her seat. "It…it no longer suits me, ma'am." Edith looked at her with an arch expression. "Since those in charge of you changed, you mean?"

Dolly Deans coloured bright red. "I eh…I only meant…" Mrs Markham laughed. "It's all right, child. I know what's been happening. I may come over as fusty old lady, but I know what's going on almost everywhere. I know your situation."

Lifting a sandwich and taking a bite, Dolly avoided replying. Mrs Markham looked at her hard. "How far did your education go?" "I reached grade eight at the Board School, ma'm," she said ,swallowing the piece of sandwich.

Mrs Markham nodded, impressed. "That is the top grade in the school, is it not?" "Yes, ma'am" said Dolly. Edith Markham smiled. "You are a remarkable and surprising young woman, Dolly Deans. So, what sort of post are you looking for?"

Leaning forward eagerly, Dolly blurted out, "Oh, anything ma'am. A maid or cook. I have no experience but I am a quick study."

Mrs Markham laughed. "A maid or a cook? I have an excellent cook and a perfectly good maid." Dolly's face fell. "Then I hope I haven't wasted your time, ma'am." The older woman stood up and walked over to a writing desk. Pulling up the roll-top cover she revealed a huge pile of letters scattered higgledy-piggledy . "I have many irons in the fire. Miss Deans. I am on the board of several charities. I have business interests. I have many meetings and social functions to attend."

Indicating the papers on the desk she said, "It is an increasing struggle to keep this avalanche under control. What I need is a private secretary to organise all this. To keep my appointments diary in order. To arrange the trivia of my life so that it does not overwhelm me. You know my health is rather fragile. I need to keep my strength for the important tasks."

Returning to her seat she looked Dolly squarely in the face. "What do you think, Miss Deans?" "Think, Mrs Markham?" The older woman smiled. "Yes, think about the position?" Dolly could not quite believe she was being offered such an elevated post.

"Me as your private secretary, ma'am? But I have no experience of such a thing."

Edith Markham brushed her comment away with a wave of her hand. "Tish and tosh. You have a good brain in your head. You are well educated.. You read and write well, you have common-sense and you are a hard worker, what else is needed?"

Taking a sip of tea she looked at Dolly. "Well, would you like to work for me, Dolly Deans?" Dolly could not believe the wonderful opportunity that had opened before her. "Oh, yes, Mrs Markham, I would be honoured."

Clapping her hands together decisively Mrs Markham stood up. "Good, that is settled. Now to practical matters. The salary is thirty shillings a week, payable fortnightly. You will get a dress allowance. You will need three different outfits, day to day, semi-formal and formal." Edith Markham went on. "Your meals will be provided, of course." Dolly could not believe her ears. It seemed like a wonderful dream.

Mrs Markham continued in a business-like manner. "Usually the hours will be nine to five, but on occasion you may need to start earlier or work later. Also, sometimes you may have to accompany me on trips that require being away overnight. That would be very rare, but it only seems fair to let you know."

Dolly felt a pang of trepidation when she heard she might sometimes be away overnight. She knew how fragile her mother's health was and leaving her alone, looking after Liza for an extended period, was worrying. But on the other hand, she thought, Mrs Markham had said it would be very rare. The advantages far outweighed any inhibitions she might have. The rise in wages would make a massive difference to the Deans family. Better food and clothes. A doctor for her mother.

"Those conditions would suit me very well, Mrs Markham." "Good," said Edith Markham briskly. "Now, when can you take up the post?" Dolly frowned. "Well, I have to give Wentlock's a month's notice. I hope that is not inconvenient."

Going over to a desk calendar Mrs Markham checked the dates. "That would be the middle of February. Monday the fourteenth. St Valentine's Day. What a nice date to start. Hearts and flowers everywhere." Dolly laughed.

"That would suit admirably, ma'am." Mrs Markham rang the little bell then held out her hand. "Then it's decided, February the fourteenth. Bright and early." Taking the proffered hand Dolly shook it firmly. "Bright and early, ma'am."

The maid appeared and showed Dolly to the front door. As she stepped onto the pavement she leaned back against the railings, unable to believe her change of fortune. Wait till her mother heard. She would also write to Thomas with the good news. It would cheer him up. All the way home on the tram she went over and over what Mrs Markham had said. Dolly felt elated. Her duties would be varied and interesting. Not like the drudgery of Wentlock's.

Thinking of the shop she smiled as she thought of the satisfaction she would get tell Miss Meredith she was leaving. Stepping off the tram she went into a fish and chip shop and bought portions for the whole family. Normally she would never been so extravagant but this was a special occasion. She also remembered to buy a piece of black pudding for Old Peggy's Dog.

Reaching the front steps the little canine leapt up eagerly to meet her. Dolly patted his head. "Hello, Old Peggy's Dog. Hope you've had a good day." She lifted the black pudding from the newspaper it was wrapped in. Holding it up she said. "What have we got here? I wonder what little bow-wow would like this?" As he caught the scent of the black pudding he spun around frantically.

Dolly teased him for a second then threw the pudding for him to catch. As he eagerly gobbled down the treat she patted his head. "For once I don't have to tell you my troubles, Old Peggy's Dog. For once things have turned out rather wonderful."

Walking into the house the family were amazed when she put the fish and chips on the table. Billy stared wide-eyed. "Blimey, sis have you robbed a bank?" Dolly laughed. While her mother fetched the plates, Dolly told them her news. All were excited by her change of fortune. When she said what her new salary would be Billy whistled aloud. "Thirty bob a week? That's more than the Queen Vicky gets, I bet." His mother pointed a warning finger. "I told you before, show respect to the queen."

Sitting round the table, all tucking in to the fish and chips the Deans family chatted more happily than they had for a long time. Little Liza sat on Dolly's knee and helped herself to large portions of flakey cod..

Just as they were finishing a knock came to the door. Billy answered. It was the post. Dolly's heart leapt when he returned with a letter for her. Even from a distance she could see it was Thomas' writing.

Snatching it from her brother she took it into the other room and read it eagerly. As usual he kept the tone light and jokey. Telling her silly stories about what went on in camp. But even Thomas could not disguise the growing casualties on both sides.

He emphasised that where he was stationed was safe, but Dolly knew this was to keep her from worrying. Near the end he told her how much he loved her and missed her and how he couldn't wait to get home so they could marry. At the bottom of the letter were a row of kisses. Dolly put the paper to her lips and kissed them in return.

Chapter Nineteen

It had been the longest month of Dolly's life. Working out her notice at Wentlock's had been excruciating. When she handed in her resignation Miss Meredith was pale with anger. Dolly suspected it was because the manageress would no longer be able to make her life a misery.

Even Mr Wentlock called her up to his office and chided her for leaving. Saying that she was showing great ingratitude after the firm had treated her so well. Dolly had tried to tell him she appreciated all he had done, but he dismissed her with a curt wave of his hand.

Now, wearing her best dress, she made her way towards the Markham house. She checked the clock on the office building. She was twenty minutes early. Knocking the door she took a deep breath and prepared for her great adventure. The maid ushered her in.

"Mrs Markham is still sleeping," the maid said. "Would you like to come down for a cup of tea till she wakes?" Dolly gave a warm smile of thanks. "That would be lovely. By the way, I'm Miss Deans. Just call me Dolly." The girl returned the smile. "And I'm Annie." Dolly held out her hand. "Pleased to meet you, Annie." The maid looked surprised for a second and then took the offered hand. She led Dolly down a set of stairs leading off the hallway. Walking along a corridor they reached a spacious kitchen. Here, sitting round a large table, were a middle-aged woman and two younger girls. All were drinking tea.

Annie announced Dolly to the group. "This is Miss Deans, Dolly, who's come to work for Mrs Markham. Dolly this is Martha". She said pointing to, a jolly-looking woman, with red cheeks "Martha is the cook." "Please to meet you, I'm sure," Martha said, smiling. "And this is Sally and Elsie" Annie went on, indicating the two younger woman. "Elsie does laundry and cleaning, and Sally is the assistant cook." The girls said shy hellos.

"I said Dolly might like a cup of tea while she waited for Mrs Markham to wake up." Martha beamed. "Of course, come and sit down, lovey." She had a warm, west country accent. Dolly sat down as the tea was poured. The cook said "Mrs Markham is usually up and about with the lark but she was a bit off-colour last night, poor thing. So she needs a good sleep."

As she drank her tea Dolly chatted with the others. All seemed nice and friendly. They were curious about her new post and very impressed by her title of private secretary.

Just as Martha was about to pour another round of tea the door opened and a severe-looking woman of about thirty, with mousy-brown hair, entered. The group went instantly quiet as her gaze fell on them. She pressed her thin lips together in a gesture of disapproval.

"Is there no work to be done?" Martha half-rose in an apologetic manner. "Mrs Markham has not risen yet, Miss Langton. We were just welcoming Miss Deans. Giving her a cup of tea while she waited."

The newcomer grimaced in disapproval and then turned to Dolly. "I'm Miss Langton. The housekeeper, Deans." Her look grew steely. "As I'm responsible for all matters within the house I will expect you to report to me when you arrive in the morning. And do the same when you leave in the evening." The cowed staff looked at each other under lowered eyes. Langton went on. "Also, I will let you know when you may eat. I keep a strict timetable and expect you to comply."

There was a moment's silence. Dolly knew this was a seminal moment. If she accepted this then she was just changing Miss Meredith for another bully. Deliberately taking a leisurely sip of tea, she looked at the housekeeper hard.

"Thank you for that *kind* welcome, Miss Langton. But just so as we do not get off on the wrong foot, or have any misunderstandings, let me make things plain." Martha and the other two looked at each other in surprise. Deliberately pouring herself another cup of tea Dolly continued. "I am directly employed to serve Mrs Markham. I answer to her and her *alone*." As she said this Langton's cheeks flushed with anger.

"I will arrive and leave as Mrs Markham wishes, and no one else." The three onlookers fought to hide their grins. Draining the last drop of tea, Dolly stood up.

"As to my meals, I will let you know when *I* wish to eat and not when you decide." There was a moment of silence before she added, "And by the way, I am *Miss* Deans, never Deans! If you wish us to be on first name terms then you may call me Dolly and I will call you by your first name. The choice is yours. But never again call me *Deans,* is that understood?"

The housekeeper looked incandescent. She seemed to be about to explode, but then left, slamming the door loudly behind her. The kitchen was in stunned silence for a moment then the rest of the staff burst into laughter.

Martha wiped her eyes. "Well, I'm blessed. I never thought I'd see such a thing." She turned to the girls. "Did you see Miss Langton's face? Like a beetroot that was about to blow up, she was."

At that moment one of the bells along the top of the wall jangled loudly. Annie looked up. "That's Mrs Markham. We can go up now." Dolly followed her upstairs. Her heart was beating fast at the exchange she had just had with Miss Langton. But she knew she had done the right thing and nipped any bullying in the bud. The maid knocked at the bedroom door and on hearing a voice entered with Dolly following.

Mrs Markham was sitting up in bed. When Annie drew back the curtains Dolly could see her employer looked pale. " I must apologise, child. I was a little unwell last night. I could not sleep so I've laid in past my time." Dolly smiled. "I'm glad you feel a little better. Is there anything I can get you?" Edith Markham sat up straighter. "No, thank you. I'll have a little breakfast and then we can get started" Turning to the maid she said, "Annie, would you tell Cook I'd like two soft boiled eggs, some toast and a pot of tea, please." With a nod Annie left.

Dolly hovered uncertainly. "Is there anything you would like me to be getting on with, Mrs Markham?" The older woman shook her head. "Plenty of time, Dolly. If you go into the drawing room and have a look through the letters I showed you, and start putting them in the order you think important, I shall join you when I have eaten and dressed. If you need anything, Miss Langton the house-keeper will be more than glad to help, I'm sure. Have you met Miss Langton?"

"Oh, yes, ma'am, I've met Miss Langton," Dolly said dryly.

Going to the drawing room Dolly opened the desk and was soon immersed in sorting through the piles of correspondence, trying to put them into categories, dates and order of importance. Time flew past and she was surprised when Mrs Markham, now fully dressed, entered the room.

"How are we doing, Dolly? she said, looking at the pile of papers heaped around the floor. "Fine, ma'am, just getting to grips with them." Mrs Markham nodded in approval. "Good, good. Now leave that for now, we are going out." "Out, ma'am?" Dolly said, looking nonplussed. "Yes, I have some shopping to do and we must also get you the dresses we promised."

Dolly felt she was dreaming when she joined Mrs Markham in a splendid coach, drawn by two white horses. She felt like Cinderella going to the ball. As carriage made its way through the city she thought, if her friends could see her now. Little Dolly Deans from Whitechapel riding like a lady.

*

They drew up outside Harrods. Dolly followed Mrs Markham inside. The store took her breath away. The size and splendour. The luxury goods. Dolly had to stop herself from gawking open-mouthed at the sights. After Edith Markham had made a few purchases they went to the clothes department. Here, three dresses were picked out for Dolly. The young east ender could not believe how lovely they were.

She tried to tell Mrs Markham they were too grand for her but her protests were waved away. As her employer spoke to the staff, arranging for delivery, Dolly looked around and spotted a familiar face. It was Miss Andrews, her old manageress from Wentlock's, whose eyes widened when she saw her ex-assistant looking so prosperous.   Dolly smiled and waved over. Miss Andrews returned the gesture

Mrs Markham concluded the delivery arrangements and they made their way back to the carriage. After a brief stop, where Dolly waited in the vehicle while her employer met her solicitor, they headed home.

*

Arriving back at the house, Dolly showed Mrs Markham the initial sorting she had done on the paperwork. The older woman was delighted. "Splendid work, Miss Deans. I have been dreading facing this. But you are already making progress."

Dolly could not help but notice Mrs Markham looked very tired. "Would you like to rest for a little while ma'am?" she said with a look of concern. Edith Markham nodded. "Perhaps I have exerted myself too soon after last night."

Looking at her sympathetically Dolly said, "A little light lunch, perhaps? Some nourishing broth, with toast soldiers." "That is a very good suggestion. I shall have it in my bedroom and then rest this afternoon. Please tell Cook what I want."

Helping her upstairs Dolly then hurried down to the kitchen. Cook was putting together a heavy meal of chops, potatoes, and dumplings, watched by Miss Langton. Martha looked up. "Just preparing Mrs Markham' lunch, Dolly, then we can have ours." She then poured a coating of thick gravy over the meal. Dolly looked at the stodgy pile on the plate. "Pardon, me, Cook, but Mrs Markham is feeling rather delicate. Perhaps some broth and toast."

At this the housekeeper exploded. "*Miss* Deans, I'll thank you to leave Mrs Markham culinary needs to me!" She glared at Dolly. "I have been here two years, you have been here five minutes! I know far more than you what's good for Mrs Markham. So I will thank you not to interfere!"

With this she put the plate of heavy food on a tray and stormed out the door. All in the kitchen looked at each other in silence for a moment. Then Martha shrugged. "Oh, well, takes all sorts, that's what I say." At this they all laughed. Plates were put out and Martha was about to serve lunch when the door flew open with a crash. An apoplectic Miss Langton stood in the doorway with the tray of food. Slamming it down on the table she glared at Martha and shouted one word. "BROTH!" before turning and storming out.

Those at the tables smothered muffled giggles. Sally dished out the food while Martha heated some broth made the day before. Toasting some slices of bread she cut them into soldiers. Putting the repast on a tray she handed it to Annie, then shouted "BROTH!" Dolly, along with all the others, collapsed helpless with laughter.

Chapter Twenty

It had been an amazing six weeks since Dolly had taken up employment with Mrs Markham Time had flown. She was very happy with how things had gone. The work was varied and interesting. Her employer was delighted with her application and entrusted her with more and more complex tasks. These duties did not keep her confined to the house. Several times a week she would accompany Mrs Markham to many of her meetings. Not only did Edith Markham have extensive business interests but she was on the board of many charities.

With her first month's wages Dolly had been able to buy warm coats for her mother, Liza and Billy. Also, for the first time in three years, the

Deans were eating well. Meat and fresh vegetables replaced scrag ends and mashed potatoes.

Dolly got on with the rest of the staff. They would all chat and joke over lunch. Life in the house was convivial except for the presence of Miss Langton. The housekeeper was the only dark shadow over the household. Since she had failed in her attempt to dominate Dolly she had took her spite out on the others. Several times she had reduced Annie, Elsie or Sally to tears.

Towards Dolly she maintained a frigid civility. Only speaking to her when absolutely necessary. This suited Dolly Deans but she wished she could do something about her treatment of the others. She knew Mrs Markham would not tolerate such behaviour if she knew. But the young private secretary did not think it was her place to tell tales about the running of the household.

Looking in her employer's social diary she saw there was an appointment in an hour for something called the NUWSS. Dolly didn't know what this was but had merely written it in the week before, after Mrs Markham left her a note.

Dolly was slightly worried that she had not received a letter from Thomas for about nine days. Usually he would write two or three time a week. Her mother reassured her that sometimes in the confusion of a war situation post could be delayed

At that moment Edith Markham came in dressed for an outing. She was looking better and her health had been steadier the past few weeks. "Good morning, Dolly," she called over. 'Morning, Mrs Markham, I hope you slept well." Her employer smiled. "Yes I did thank you. Nothing like a good night's sleep. What was it Shakespeare said 'sleep that knits up the ravelled sleeve of care.' "

Smiling, Dolly said, "My mum says much the same thing, ma'am. A good sleep does you the world of good." Mrs Markham laughed. "Your mother and Shakespeare are in agreement I see."

Checking the diary Dolly said. "You have a meeting in an hour, ma'am. With the NUWSS."

Mrs Markham nodded. "Yes. Yes, I know. I should like you to come along, Dolly. To take notes.   And I also think you will find it very interesting."

*

As the carriage trundled through London Dolly's curiosity got the better of her. "Pardon me for asking, Mrs Markham, but what is the NUWSS?"   Edith Markham   smiled. "How remiss of me, I just assumed you knew. The NUWSS stands for the National Union of Women's Suffrage Societies."

Dolly look puzzled "Suffrage, ma'am?" "Yes, votes for women." Furrowing her brows in puzzlement her young assistant continued, "But women don't have the vote, Mrs Markham."

"Yes, and that's why we're campaigning, child," Edith Markham said with a chuckle. "This is the twentieth century. We will not be silenced anymore. We will have the vote."

Dolly pondered this new idea. She had never thought of women having the vote before, always assuming that only men having the vote was the natural state of things. She found the idea of women demanding the vote breathtakingly bold.

*

The carriage pulled up outside a large hall in the centre of London. Dolly followed Mrs Markham inside. To her amazement the place was packed with several hundred women. Many carried banners demanding equality. There was an air of excitement in the air. Edith Markham was a member of the committee and was led up to the platform to join the others. Before this, she told Dolly to take a note of any important motions made.

Sitting in the front row Dolly's curiosity grew. Who were these women? They looked ordinary and respectable but she sensed a spirt of rebellion. As chairwoman Mrs Markham welcomed the audience, said a few words about the cause, and then introduced the leader of their movement, Millicent Fawcett.

There was thunderous applause as a small, middle-aged woman rose to speak. As she outlined the case for equality of the vote Dolly grew more interested. She had never heard such inspiring words. When the speech was finished the audience rose to their feet in thunderous applause.

Dolly Deans felt elated. It was as if the scales had fallen from her eyes. Why shouldn't women have the vote, it was their world too? As she stood, inspired by the cheering women around her, she decided she would join the fight.

*

On the way back in the carriage she talked excitedly to Mrs Markham who was delighted that she was joining the association. Arriving at the house, Dolly climbed out. Annie and Sally brought out Mrs Markham luggage. She was spending a weekend in the country with friends.

Before she left she told Dolly that, as she would not be back till Monday, she could take whole weekend off. This delighted the young east ender. Two days with the family and her friend, Millie.

After her employer left Dolly went into the study to tackle a job Mrs Markham had asked to her take care of. The household accounts had not been balanced properly for almost eighteen months. Edith Markham declared herself neglectful. It was a task she did assiduously in the past but bouts of poor health and a full schedule had led her to let things slip.

Dolly collected the large account books, plus bundles of receipts and bills from the various tradespeople. For the next hour or so she checked outgoings for goods and services. When she finished she shook her head in disbelief.

213

That could not be right. She thought she must have made a mistake.

Checking again, step by step, comparing every bill with household expenditure, she was stunned to reach the same total. Even though the figures could not lie, the result had such repercussions that Dolly went through the process for the third time.

At last she slumped back in the chair. There was no mistake. When Mrs Markham returned on Monday the awful truth would have to be told.

Chapter Twenty One

Re-reading the letter Dolly was torn between relief and worry. When she got home on Friday night it had been waiting. The tone and style was so different from the missives Thomas had been writing previously. It was short, with the handwriting scrawled rather than his usual the neat style. The paper was also crumpled as if the letter had been written under adverse conditions.

More worrying for Dolly was the fact that for the first time Thomas wrote about the war in much more graphic terms. He told of fierce fighting and many casualties. The young soldier still made the effort to keep up her spirits by say they expected a big push any day that would bring the conflict to a swift end.

She wiped away a tear as her mother entered. "What's the matter, love?" Dolly held up the letter. "I'm so afraid, mum." Mrs Deans gave her daughter hug. "It will be all right. The papers all say it will be over soon." Dolly let out a snort of derision. "Those same papers all said it would be over by Christmas." Giving her daughter a hug Mrs Deans shook her head sadly. "Such a terrible waste. Such a terrible waste."

Dolly took Liza out for a walk. The little girl loved being with her sister. Taking her to Victoria Park they had a lovely time feeding the ducks with the slices of bread they had brought along. It was too chilly to stay long in the open air so they went into a little café   and had buttered toast and tea. When Liza had eaten her fill they returned home.

*

" Just going to see Millie, mum," Dolly called over her shoulder as she closed the door. She hurried along Whitechapel High Street, really looking forward to seeing her friend. She needed not only to talk about Thomas, but also what she had discovered.

She reached the shop and was impressed by what Millie had done since she had last been there. The exterior was painted in bold red and gold, catching the eye of anyone passing by. There was also a new sign, professionally

217

painted, which said ,'Millie's Bakery. The Best in Whitechapel.'

Dolly smiled at this. Her friend could never be accused of hiding her light under a bushel. Going in, Millie was behind the counter. There was also a young girl, with an apron, arranging loaves on the shelves.

Her friend beamed with delight. "Well, look who it is. Miss Too Posh for Whitechapel Now." Dolly laughed. "The shop looks wonderful. When did you start selling bread?" Millie shrugged. "Well, people buy bread more than they buy cakes. So, I read Mrs Beeton again and now I sell bread as well." The baker indicated to Dolly to come behind the counter. They stepped into the bakery. Dolly saw another young girl kneading dough. "Is that two people you have working for you?" she asked in amazement.

Grinning Millie said,. "Well, I can't do everything myself. So, what's going on?" Dolly said, "I found something and I need your advice."

*

They sat in the small back room of the bakery. Millie took a deep swig of tea. "That is a bit of something troublesome. Very troublesome." Sighing, Dolly said, "I know. I know what I should do but it will cause such an awful situation. What do you think I should do, Mill?"

Millie looked hard at her. "Has Mrs Markham been good to you?" "Of course."

"Does she deserve your loyalty?" "Of course," Dolly blurted out. "Then, Dolly Deans," her friend said, looking her squarely in the eye, "you already know what you must do."

Chapter Twenty Two

There was an uncomfortable silence. The only sound heard was the heavy ticking of the Ormolu clock on the mantelpiece. Dolly looked at Mrs Markham. Her face had been mask of stone when she told her what she had discovered. They had both gone over the figures again. There was no mistake. On a small table were the account books. There was a soft tap at the door of the drawing room. Miss Langton entered. She looked from Mrs Markham to Dolly and back again.

"You wished to see me, Mrs Markham?" The lady of the house stared hard at Langton until the housekeeper began to squirm uncomfortably. Eventually she broke the silence. "Is there anything wrong, Madam?"

Dolly lowered her eyes. The tension was unbearable. Finally Mrs Markham spoke. "Do you know the definition of cheat. Miss Langton?" The woman grimaced uncertainly. "Cheat? I...I'm not sure what you mean, Mrs Markham?"

Edith Markham raised her voice. "The definition of cheat is to act dishonestly to gain advantage." Miss Langton bridled up. "I really don't know why I am being asked..." She was cut off in full flow by Mrs Markham indicating the accounts books. "There is all the evidence we need, madam, of your systematic swindling." Langton raised her eyes in indignation. "I did not come here to..." Mrs Markham pointed an angry finger at her. "Just one word, madam, just one false protestation of innocence and I shall send for a constable and have you arrested." The housekeeper's lower lip began to tremble and her eyes grew teary.

" Since you have been here you have been overcharging me on countless items. Sixpence here, a shilling there. But all have added up the more than a hundred and twenty pounds. And if it wasn't for Miss Deans no doubt you would have gone on robbing me." At the mention of Dolly's name the housekeeper shot her a malevolent glance.

Mrs Markham glared at the hapless housekeeper. "I am still of a mind to have you charged by the police." At this Miss Langton's face crumpled into a mask of anguish. Tears rolled down her cheeks. "Please, Mrs Markham, not the police. I beg you." Taking out a handkerchief she dabbed at her eyes. "It was weakness nothing more. I am not a criminal by nature. I just allowed myself to be overcome by temptation."

Taking a deep breath to control her sobs she went on. "I will pay the money back. I have it at the Post Office Savings Bank. I could let you have it in an hour." Although she knew Langton to be a spiteful and unpleasant woman. Dolly could not help but feel pity for her. To have fallen so far. She would never hold a respectable position again.

Her employer contemplated the pathetic figure before her for a few moments then made a decision. "Very, well, here is what you will do. You return the money you stole. Then you will have an hour to pack your belongings and leave this house." She went on. "Needless to say you will do so without a reference. Now go and retrieve the money. That is all."

Gabbling her thanks Miss Langton backed out of the room. Edith Markham looked at Dolly, a sad expression on her face. "So tragic. A reputation, a life, thrown away for a few pounds."

Chapter Twenty Three

Dolly, holding up a banner, marched past the Houses of Parliament with several hundred other women of the NUWSS. In the weeks following her first meeting she had become an enthusiastic advocate of women's right to vote. Her mother was astounded when she came home and expounded her belief, thinking her daughter had taken leave of her senses.

But Dolly was committed to the justness of the cause. She would pass out leaflets and debate the subject at the drop of a hat. Millie was amazed at the change in her friend. She was no longer little Dolly Deans of Whitechapel but a confident young woman, growing more sophisticated with the passing weeks.

Much of this was due to the influence of Edith Markham who encouraged her not only to become active in the cause of suffrage, but to read a wide range of books covering science, politics and literature.

As it was Sunday, when the rally was over, Dolly jumped on a tram and made her way back to Whitechapel. She was anxious to get home, hoping for a letter from Thomas. It had been more two weeks since she had last heard from him. Running past Old Peggy's Dog, who looked at her hopefully, she burst into the room. "Hello, mum. Any letters?" Mrs Deans shook her head. "Sorry, love. Nothing."

Dolly felt a sinking feeling in the pit of her stomach. If he was all right Thomas would have written

***

Poring over Mrs Markham's Monday post Dolly tried to drive the worry about Thomas from her mind. Despite her mother's attempts to comfort her she would not find peace until she heard from him.

One consolation was that the household much had changed for the better. Since the dismissal of Langton there had been a moving around of the staff. Martha, the cook, had been promoted to housekeeper on Dolly's recommendation. Sally was now the cook, Elsie her assistant, and a new girl taken on as laundress and cleaner.

It was a measure of how much Mrs Markham had grown to rely on Dolly that she had left the entire reorganization to her. Intermittent bouts of ill-health had often left her incapacitated., so the support of her young assistant proved invaluable.

As she was finishing the post Mrs Markham came in. "Ah, Dolly, here you are. Anything of vital importance in the mail?" Dolly smiled. "Nothing to call out the fire brigade for, Mrs Markham." The older woman chuckled. "Good. What time is the meeting at the National War Aid Society?"

Checking the diary, Dolly said. "Eleven o' clock." Her employer frowned. "Oh, how unfortunate. I have a vital meeting with my legal advisor. Too important to miss."

Mrs Markham was one of the committee who decided on the merits of the cases of those who sought help. Funds were allocated on the basis of individual hardship. The society also sent boxes to the front, with warm clothes, tobacco and sweets.

The Aid Society was a cause close to Dolly's heart. It was set up to help the soldiers and their families who struggled in the war. She liked to think that if Thomas ever needed help someone would be kind to him.

Looking enquiringly at Mrs Markham Dolly asked,. "Shall I send your apologies?" Edith Markham shook her head. "No, people are depending on us. You go. I shall phone Margaret Hawkins and tell her you are there in my place."

"Me, ma'am? But I have never done that sort of thing before," Dolly said. Mrs Markham waved away her protest. "Nonsense. I can think of no one I trust more."

*

The stories were heart breaking. Dolly sat at a table and interviewed the wives of soldiers who had either been killed in the war, or had come back with terrible injuries. Filling in the forms as poor souls asked for help she wished she could just give each a handful of money, but the charity demanded a means-test form was filled and then passed on for scrutiny to another committee.

As the afternoon drew on Dolly felt that she could not listen to one more story of misery. The one thought that kept her going was that she would treat each applicant as she would like Thomas' family to be treated.

There was one light moment when she called the next in line. As the woman stood up Dolly recognized her as Mary Phillips, an old classmate of hers. Mary was known as trickster and thief. She was no soldier's wife. The two children she had brought along were obviously not hers. In fact she was not even married. Phillips face fell as she recognised Dolly. She turned and hurried from the room.

Dolly made a mental note to warn the other volunteers about Mary Phillips. At last the

afternoon ended. Dolly handed it the forms and
made her way back to report to Mrs Markham.

*

Knocking at the front door Dolly felt tired.
Her fingers ached from writing for several
hours. As soon as Annie opened the door she
could see by the girl's face something was amiss.
"Annie, what's wrong?" The maid's eyes were
tearful. "Oh, Dolly, it's Mrs Markham. She's
been taken ever so bad!"

Rushing past her Dolly raced upstairs.
Bursting into the bedroom she saw an ashen-
looking Mrs Markham lying on the bed while
the doctor took her pulse. The ill woman looked
up and smiled weakly. "Dolly, I hope things
went well. I'm sorry I couldn't be there." The

233

physician frowned at her disapprovingly. "This is no time to be worrying about other things, Mrs Markham. I have told you many times you must take life easier and not overstrain your heart."

Dolly hurried over to the bed. Edith Markham looked so small and vulnerable. Not like the strong and energetic person she usually was. Taking her hand she said. "Everything went well, Mrs Markham." The ill woman smiled. "Good. Good." The doctor looked at his patient sternly. " I will write you out a prescription which must be filled at once. Take one of these tablets three times a day." He closed his bag with a click. "Now, rest and nothing but rest and we'll soon have you well."

Handing the prescription to Dolly he said. "Have this filled at once. And make sure she follows my orders." Dolly nodded. When the doctor left she sent Annie to the chemist while she had the kitchen make up some clear soup.

When this arrived she coaxed Mrs Markham into finishing the whole bowl. Her employer looked at the clock "It's past your time, Dolly. You must go home." Shaking her head the younger woman said "I'll stay with you Mrs Markham, just till you feel a little better." The stricken woman protested weakly but Dolly could see in her eyes she was grateful.

*

The afternoon light faded into darkness. Dolly sat in a chair by the bedside, reading to Mrs

Markham one her favourite books. The carriage clock on the bedside table struck eight. Mrs Markham turned to the younger woman. " I am feeling a little better. You should go now." She had in fact regained a little of her colour but Dolly sensed she was not yet ready to be left alone.

Closing the book she said, "I'll sit with you a while longer, ma'am. I don't mind. We'll have tea and a fancy cake in a little while, shall we? A proper treat." Mrs Markham smiled. "Yes, that would be a proper treat." After a moment she said. "Have you heard from your young man?" Dolly shook her head. "No, ma'am. I must confess I'm growing worried."

"I'm sure he will be well. In a while this dreadful war will be over and you'll be together. Love is the most important thing, love is the *only* thing that matters."

Mrs Markham looked at her sadly. " I found love once, Dolly, *real* love but I listened to other people and let it slip through my fingers." Dolly looked at her in puzzlement. "But why didn't you marry your love? Edith Markham sighed deeply. "He was considered not quite 'one of us,' at least that's what my father and mother said."

Dolly's heart went out to her in her sorrow. "But couldn't you have just defied them, ma'am?" Edith smiled sadly. " I was young. I didn't have the courage or the strength to defy my parents. So, I let him go. I married a man, a good man, a 'suitable' man but I never loved him in the way I did John. That was his name. She took Dolly's hands in hers. " So, Dolly Deans, when your young man comes home, hold on to him, you hold on to him tight and *never* let him go.

Chapter Twenty Four

Dolly slumped into the chair. She was very tired. In the three weeks since Mrs Markham had taken ill she had not only been carrying out all her duties, but also overseeing the running of the household. Her employer was making a good recovery but was not yet up to the day to day tasks. On top of that was the constant worry about no word from Thomas.

Liza came over and waved the little dancing monkey in her face. Dolly laughed. She pointed to the toy. "That's one cheeky little monkey," then she pointed to Liza, "and that's two cheeky little monkeys." The little girl gurgled with delight.

Mrs Deans looked over from the stove. "Dinner will be ready soon, love. Nice stew. Do you the world of good." At that moment there was an urgent rap at the door. Mother and daughter looked at each other. As the knocking was repeated Dolly answered. Standing there were Thomas' mother and father. Mrs Turner looked as if she had been crying.

"Mr and Mrs Turner, come in." They stepped inside. The man had a letter in his hand. "We've had a letter from the Department of War." Dolly felt a chill of fear down her spine. Thomas' father continued. "It seems there was an outbreak of fever in the army. Real bad. Thomas caught it. He's been very ill." At this his wife whimpered.

Dolly took her arm. "Please, sit down, Mrs Turner." She led her to a chair at the table before turning to the man. "Thomas is very ill?" He nodded. "Yes, the letter says the infection is so severe they don't know how long it would take him and the others to recover properly, so they're being honourably discharged and sent home."

A flood of relief swept through Dolly. He was alive. He was coming home. The thought of Thomas' lying very ill in an army hospital, thousands of miles from home was heart-breaking, but at least there was light at the end of the tunnel.

Looking at Mr Turner she asked, "Does it say when he's coming home?" Mrs Turner looked up. "Just said as soon as they can get a ship. They'll let us know." Exhaling with relief Dolly said, "I'm so happy. He'll be home soon and we can get him well."

After Mrs and Mrs Turner left Dolly burst into tears . Mrs Deans held her daughter and gently shushed her. "There, love, there. No time for tears. Time to be strong. Thomas will need you to be strong."

**

When Dolly went to work the next morning, to her surprise, Mrs Markham was up and about. The three weeks of resting had done her good and she looked more like her old self. When she was told the news of Thomas Edith Markham beamed with delight.

"That is wonderful news. I' m so glad." Dolly smiled. "And I am. But I'm a bit worried about his health. They said the fever is very bad." Her employer waved away her fears. "Oh, tish tosh, he's young and strong. He'll soon recover."

This reassured Dolly and she went about the business of the day. As she began to transcribe Mrs Markham notes her employer watched her carefully. "You know it seems so antiquated, the way we have to write out everything in copperplate. Almost like medieval scribes, don't you think?" she asked. Dolly grinned. "Well, I don't think there's any other way to do it, Mrs Markham." The older woman jabbed her finger towards her. "But there is, child. I saw a typewriting machine and it's the future!" Her assistant looked perplexed. "A typewriting machine?" "Yes, I saw one at my solicitor Mr Hawkins office. A wonderful invention. I meant to tell you about it to earlier, but then my wretched illness laid me low."

Dolly wondered if Mrs Markham was still unwell. "What does it do? This typewriting machine, ma'am?" Her employer spread her arms. "You put a sheet of paper in, you press lots of little discs and you can print anything you like, neat as ninepence and as clear as day. No more endless handwriting."

She couldn't imagine a machine that could replace handwriting. Mrs Markham went on. "I shall phone my solicitor this very instant and have him order a machine." Looking at her uncertainly Dolly said, "But we would not know how to operate such a contraption." "Oh, tish tosh, the young woman in his office could not be any cleverer than you. If she could master the machine then so could Dolly Deans."

**

The next morning, as Dolly arrived, a smartly-dressed young woman with glasses and red hair sat with Mrs Markham. At her feet was what looked like a small luggage case. "Dolly, this is Miss Davis from Mr Hawkins office. Miss Davis, this is Miss Deans, my private secretary. Dolly, Mr Hawkins has kindly loaned Miss Davis for the day." The young women shook hands. "Now, Miss Davis, a demonstration if you please."

245

Putting the case on the desk she opened it to reveal a typewriter. Dolly stared at it curiously. A strange looking device with lots of little round dots which had letters and numbers and a long carriage which ran from end to end. Miss Davis took out a sheet of blank paper, rolled it into the machine and then tapped briskly on the keys. She indicated to that they should read.

Dolly could not believe her eyes. There, in proper printing; like she would see in a book, it said 'Hello Miss Deans, I am very happy to meet you.'

*

The day had been fascinating for Dolly. Miss Davis showed her the basic functions of the typewriter and explained how to change the ribbon. Dolly was particularly taken by the use of carbon paper copies. She had spent a lot of time tediously writing out the same letter twice.

After she thought she had the basics Miss Davis invited her to sit at the machine. Then, encouraged by the typist, she slowly picked out her name. She could not believe that she had actually achieved this. After another hour of effort Miss Davis rose to go.

"Now, Miss Deans, it will take lots of practise before you can type at any speed. But now you know how it's done I'm sure you'll get on splendidly.'

When she was left alone Dolly ploddingly kept typing her name. By near the end of the afternoon she felt confident enough to try a whole sentence. Her brow furrowed in concentration. Painstakingly slowly she tapped out the message. When she was finished she sat back and looked proudly at what she had typed. 'My name is Dolly Deans and I live in Whitechapel.'

She stared at the paper in wonder. How far she had come in such a short while.

Chapter Twenty Five

Her heart beat with excitement as she stood among the crowds milling about Waterloo Station. It seemed an eternity to Dolly before Thomas's parents were informed when he would arrive back in England. The area was packed with anxious, crying wives, sweethearts and parents seeing their loved ones off to war.

Dolly and Thomas' mum and dad, were in the other group waiting impatiently to meet those coming home. The train was late, which added to the agonising anticipation. Dolly stopped a porter.

"Excuse me. What time will the Southampton train be in?" He looked at her and smiled. "There it is now, Miss." Dolly turned to see a distant plume of steam approaching platform eight.

There was a surge as others waiting for their loved ones rushed to the gate. The great locomotive hissed to a halt. The crowd was pushed back as the ticket collectors needed room to open the barrier. The first men began to disembark. They all wore khaki uniforms, some torn and stained. Many were injured and were helped by their friends.

Finally Dolly saw a familiar figure moving slowly towards her. Thomas waved and smiled. She could not contain herself. Rushing past the protesting ticket collectors she threw herself into his arms. "Thomas. Thomas. Thomas," she repeated through her tears. He held her tight, kissing her on the top of the head and then gently on the lips. Looking at him more closely Dolly could see he was painfully thin. His face was gaunt and drawn. Hugging him close they walked to the barrier.

His mother, crying and laughing at the same time, threw her arms around his neck. Mr Turner wiped his eyes with a handkerchief. "Must have a bit of a cold coming," he said somewhat hoarsely. Holding out his hand he said "Welcome home, boy."

The happy quartet made their way out of the station where Dolly insisted they took a cab. On the way home Thomas spoke a little about the war, but Dolly sensed it was not something he wanted to dwell on. So she brought him up to date with all her news. He was delighted to hear how well she was doing.

When they reached the Turner house in Whitechapel they all fussed around the returning warrior. Mrs Turner, in particular, insisted he sit by the fire while she made him one of his favourite treats, buttered toast. Thomas looked at Dolly and winked. She could tell he, like her, wanted some time alone.

Finally he stood up. "I'd like to go to the Castle Alley baths, mum. I've haven't been out of this uniform for weeks." His mother immediately offered to go with him. Mr Turner looked at the two young people. "No, let Dolly take him, mother. Give you a chance to get things ready here." Dolly gave him a smile of gratitude. Thomas' father winked in return.

"Could you bundle up my street clothes, mum.?" Thomas said, " After I bathe I don't want to put on this dirty uniform again." His mother packed his apparel in a bag which Dolly insisted on carrying. Arm in arm they made their way along Whitechapel High Street. Thomas looked around. "You know, I never realised how much this place means to me, Dolly. In that strange land, with all sorts of beautiful scenery and exotic animals, all I could think about was getting home to dirty, shabby old Whitechapel and the girl I love."

*

Dolly waited in the foyer until he came out of the bathhouse. He looked more like his old self out of uniform, although she could see he was still quite weak. But the bath had

freshened him up and taken the tattered look from him. Taking his arm she said "What about you and me going for a big slap-up meal of bangers and mash." Thomas laughed. "Bangers and mash. I must be in heaven."

Making their way to a café just off the High Street they ordered their meal. Dolly could tell the smell of cooking must be tantalising to Thomas after months of army rations. She reached across and touched his hand. "How are you feeling?" Thomas smiled. "All the better for being with you. I missed you so, Dolly."

The food arrived and she was glad to see him eat with a healthy appetite. They spoke little until they were finished. Thomas took a deep drink from the mug of mahogany-brown tea the waitress brought. "That's better," he said, "Couldn't get a decent cuppa for love nor money in the army."

She could see he was making a real effort to be cheerful but the strain was written on his face. "So, what happens now?" she asked. Thomas grinned. "Now I order another mug of tea." Dolly slapped him playfully on the wrist. "You great fool. You know what I mean. When you're better are you going back to the police?"

He nodded. "Of course. It's a job I love. I'll be back on the beat as soon as I can."

"How quickly can you do that?"

"Well, that depends on how soon I can get back on my feet properly."

She was glad he was sounding so positive. Her greatest fear was that the horrors of war might have changed his nature.

Wiping a drop of tea from his upper lip with her hanky Dolly said, "Who decides you're ready?" He shrugged. "Obviously the police doctor. When I think I'm fighting fit I go there for an examination and if I pass then I'm back on the force."

After they finished Dolly paid the bill. Thomas, to his embarrassment ,found he had no money. On their way back they stopped and looked in the shop windows. In one was a splendid bridal gown. They both stared for a moment then Thomas turned to her. "Dolly Deans, will you marry me?" She smiled. "Of course I've already agreed when I took the ring." "But I mean soon." "How soon?"

He held her by lightly by the shoulders. "When I was over there, I thought I might die. But I told myself if I was spared I wouldn't waste a minute of my life. And the most important thing in my life is you. So let's get married as quickly as we can."

Chapter Twenty Six

It had been quite a while since Dolly had Sunday tea with Miss Burgess and she was looking forward to seeing her old headmistress. They had always kept in touch, but the events of the last year had taken up so much of Dolly's time. So she was delighted to receive a note in her teacher's neat handwriting inviting her to visit.

Miss Burgess lived in Hackney, in one of a row of cottages that had once been built for railwaymen. The district was a couple of miles from Whitechapel. But, as it was a fine spring morning, Dolly decided to walk.

As she made her way her mind was full of Thomas' proposal that they marry as soon as they could. The thought was thrilling. It seemed to her that they had come through so much that, as Thomas said, they did not waste any more time. They had decided they would not tell anyone yet, but would wait until they had chosen a date. But Dolly thought she would burst unless she shared her news with someone, so had decided on the way home she would confide in Millie, the one person in the world who would keep her secret.

The head-teacher's house had a trim little front garden with a bower of roses around the entrance. The hedges were neatly trimmed and the front door was painted bright red. Dolly always thought the exterior reflected her teacher perfectly. Neat and cheerful.

She rang the doorbell and the door was opened immediately by Miss Burgess who gave her a welcoming smile. "Dolly Deans, so lovely to see you. Come in. Come in." Dolly walked into the living room. Like the outside of the house it was precise and tidy.

Already laid out on the table was a fine spread of sandwiches and scones. Dolly sat down and Miss Burgess poured the tea. They brought each other up to date with what had been happening in their lives. The teacher was amazed at what had occurred to her ex-pupil over the past year. She was particularly impressed by her transition from shop assistant to private secretary. Nodding approvingly she said, "I always knew you had the brains to go far, Dolly. It was a great loss to teaching that you could not take up the offer of training"

Taking a bite of scone Dolly nodded in agreement. "Yes, Miss Burgess, it's something I would have loved to do, but , as you know, family circumstances made it impossible."

"You know I have recently learned of a charitable organisation that makes grants for educational purposes," Miss Burgess said. "I wonder if it might be worth contacting them?" Dolly smiled gratefully. "Thank you, Miss Burgess, to train as a teacher would be wonderful, but in my present position I don't think it's possible."

The teacher poured her another cup of tea. "Well, who knows what the future might bring?

I don't see any harm in inquiring, do you?"
Dolly smiled. "I don't suppose so."

"Then I will. Perhaps nothing will come of it,
but, as they say, nothing ventured nothing
gained"

**

On her way back to Whitechapel Dolly was deep
in thought. The chat with Miss Burgess had
given her much to ponder. In her heart of hearts
she would have loved to have been a teacher,
but her father's death had made that dream
impossible.

Even if she got a grant to study there was the
question of her loyalty to Miss Markham.
Without her help and kindness she would still be
a drudge at Wentlock's, under the tender

mercies of Miss Meredith. But more than that her employer had widened her horizons, taught her things, given her confidence. Dolly thought that no matter how much she would love to teach she owed Miss Markham loyalty.

So deep in thought was she that she almost strolled past Millie's bakery. Walking into the shop she was surprised at the queue of people waiting. Dolly could see that business was obviously brisk. Her friend was behind the counter, alongside another young girl serving.

Millie gave her a cheerful wave and indicated she come into the back shop. In the bakery Dolly saw two other girls working at the ovens. She looked at her friend in surprise. "You have *three* girls working for you now?" "Business is good. That second shop isn't too far away."

She led Dolly into the small back room and put the kettle on. "So, Dolly Deans, to what do I owe the honour?" Her friend put out the teacups. "I've just been to see Miss Burgess." Oh, right. She was very nice but she didn't like me." Dolly's eyes opened in surprise. "What makes you think she didn't like you?" Pouring out the tea Millie said "Well, she let all the others take turns at filling the ink-wells but not me." Dolly laughed so loud she spluttered out her tea. "That's because the one time she did, you stood behind her back pretending to drink the bottle of ink. The class were in hysterics."

They both roared with laughter at the recollection. Then Dolly looked at her friend seriously. "Thomas and I have decided to get married." "Of course you have you're engaged, " Millie snorted. "No, as soon as we can. In not more than a year." Her friend hugged her tightly. "I'm so delighted for you, Dolly. You were made for each other."

There was silence for a moment then Millie stood up. "And I'll make your wedding cake on two conditions." "Two conditions", Dolly asked curiously.

"Yes, that I'm the bridesmaid." Dolly smiled. "Done. And the other condition?"

"That for best man Thomas chooses a handsome devil.

Chapter Twenty Seven

Dolly's fingers flew across the keys of the typewriter. In the weeks that followed her first attempts she had become more and more proficient. Mrs Markham was most impressed to see how quickly she had picked up the skill.

Life was at last going well. In the past three months Thomas seemed to have turned a corner with his health. He was so sure of his recovery that he was arranged a medical examination for the following week.

After his proposal, outside the dress shop, she and Thomas had decided they would marry as soon as possible, but wait until he was fully well and had once again established himself on the force The decision to wed had given Dolly lots of things to consider. Her mum, Billy and Liza still needed her. So any wedding would need to be planned with them in mind.

They set a provisional date for a year's time. Dolly was earning a good wage and thought that she would save as much as she could in that year so that she could still help support her family after she as married. Thomas was in full agreement. Hopefully, by then, Billy would have a more settled job and contribute more.

At that moment Mrs Markham came in. She wore a coat. "Good morning, Dolly." "Good morning Mrs Markham," Dolly said in return. "Are you going out?" Edith Markham tied a scarf stylishly about her neck. "Yes, to Fortnum and Mason's. Order some hampers for a shooting weekend. I'm meeting my sisters there, then we'll have lunch at the Café Royal, probably."

Dolly looked surprised, "Your sisters, ma'am, I didn't know you had sisters." Checking her bag Mrs Markham said, "Oh, yes, I have two sisters. Eunice and Elizabeth. I have a brother, too, James. He lives in Scotland."

Standing up Dolly said "Shall I arrange the carriage?" The older woman shook her head. "No, thank you, I shall take the tram." "The tram, Mrs Markham, are you sure?" Edith Markham laughed. "Don't look so shocked. I have used the tram before. I just think it would make a nice change, a little adventure." Dolly grinned. "Alright, ma'am. I hope you enjoy the tram ride. The view from upstairs is better."

"Thank you, Dolly, I shall take your advice."

*

After Mrs Markham left Dolly got down to her daily tasks. Sorting correspondence, settling bills, filling in her employer's social diary. She was so immersed in her work that the hours flew past. Looking up at the clock she saw that it was nearly her finishing time. At that moment she heard the front door and then voices rising.

She hurried out to find Mrs Markham in the hallway. There was a cab driver and Martha helping support her. "What's happened?" Dolly asked, rushing over. "It's Mrs Markham, she's been taken poorly again," the housekeeper said anxiously. Dolly could see her employer was white and shaking. "Right, we must get her upstairs and into bed then fetch the doctor." The ailing woman tried feebly to walk. "I'm alright. Just a little turn, that's all." Her objections were brushed aside, Dolly and Martha, with the assistance of the cab driver, helped her up to the bedroom.

After paying off the driver Dolly helped Mrs Markham into bed. She then went downstairs and phoned the doctor. While waiting with the patient she poured her a little watered brandy. It seemed to bring some of the colour back to her cheeks. "Do you feel a little better ma'am? Dolly asked concernedly. Edith Markham took a tired breath. " Perhaps. I had just left my sisters, I was going to catch a tram, I did enjoy the journey out, then I suddenly felt my heart

beat so fast and I thought |I was going to faint."
Dolly gave her another little sip of brandy.
"Fortunately, a kind lady and gentleman saw I
was in distress and hailed me a cab."

At that moment the doctor arrived. He
checked her pulse and then listened to her heart.
Dolly didn't like the concern written on his face.
He blew out his cheeks. "Well, Mrs Markham,
as I've warned you many times before, your
heart is weak. You should confine yourself to a
sedentary life. Lots of rest. Nourishing food.
Avoid excitement."

Edith Markham looked at him, a faint smile on
her face. "To live like that, doctor," she said in a
weak voice," I might just a well be an exhibit in
Madame Tussaud's Waxworks." Dolly couldn't

help but grin. The physician, however, did not find it funny.

"I'll prescribe some stronger pills. They should ease any discomfort. You also need a nurse. I'll arrange for one to be with you in the morning. In the meantime is there anyone who could sit with you?" Dolly stepped forward. "I will sit with her tonight, doctor." The man nodded "Good. Good. Now please get this prescription filled immediately." "Let me show you out, doctor." Leading him downstairs she walked to the front door with the physician. As he was leaving she looked at him anxiously. "She will get better, won't she doctor?" He sighed. "Her heart is failing. She is very ill." Dolly felt herself tremble. "Yes, but with rest and good food she will recover?"

He stared at her for a few seconds. "Make sure you get those pills tonight."

Chapter Twenty Eight

She felt exhausted. After sitting up all night Dolly waited until the doctor arrived with a nurse. The physician gave orders on the treatment. Although she knew Mrs Markham needed professional medical help Dolly Deans still felt guilty about leaving her in the hands of strangers.

Edith Markham was given a strong sedative and drifted off to sleep. The doctor told Dolly the patient would not wake for some hours so she should go get some rest. Reluctantly she left the house and made her way back to Whitechapel. All the way on the tram she felt a deep feeling of fear in the pit of her stomach. She could not contemplate anything happening to Mrs Markham. A woman to whom she owed so much.

Before going to her own house she stopped off to see Thomas. He was at home, his mother and father were visiting friends. Thomas could see immediately she was in distress. "What's the matter?" he said anxiously. Dolly sat down. "It's Mrs Markham, she's very ill." Thomas stroked her hair. "Don't worry, love, she's been like this before. She'll get better I'm sure." "She's never been like this," she said tearfully, "the doctor doesn't think...doesn't think..." At this Dolly broke down and cried in his arms.

After a few minutes she regained composure. She tried to smile. "Sorry, Thomas. Just upset. Tired as well." He looked at her sympathetically. "How about a nice cup of tea and I'll tell you some good news." Dolly wiped away the tears. "Good news?" "Yes," he said, "My medical check. I just got letter this morning. I passed with flying colours. I'm back on the force next week. I was coming round to tell you when you got home." Dolly hugged him close. She needed a piece of good news very badly.

**

After a few hours sleep she made her way back to the Markham house. Knocking the door she said a silent little prayer. The door was opened by a sobbing Sally. "Oh, Dolly, it's Mrs Markham, she's gone."

**

Standing around the living room were various family members. As soon as she arrived and learned the news Dolly had looked in Edith Markham's address book and sent telegrams to her two sisters and her brother. Annie entered with a tea trolley. Following, Dolly helped her offer the beverage around the room. Elizabeth and Eunice were unmistakeable as the deceased woman's sisters. There was a striking family resemblance .

The taller of the two siblings, Eunice Webb, came over to Dolly. "Miss Deans, we'd like to thank you again for what you've done in informing us and making these arrangements." As she spoke Dolly could see even more the resemblance to Mrs Markham. Even Eunice's intonation and mannerism echoed her.

"It was the least I could do" Dolly murmured. "Mrs Markham was the kindest and most generous person I've ever met." Eunice smiled. "She spoke about you a great deal. Told us how much she had grown to rely on you and how she considered you not only a private secretary but also a friend."

Dolly felt tears welling in her eyes and took a deep breath. "Thank you, Mrs Webb. That means a great deal to me." Eunice touched Dolly's hand gently. "And thank you for being her friend." Looking around the room she went on, "Now, there are arrangements to be made after the funeral. The house. The furnishings. Such a sad duty but these things need to be done." Looking sympathetically at Dolly she said, "I'm afraid this will mean changes for yourself and the rest of the staff."

Chapter Twenty Nine

The funeral had taken place two days earlier. Dolly had been amazed at the huge amount of mourners. Not only the family, but people well known in society. The numbers had been swelled by several dozen members of the NUWSS, who turned out in black sashes.

Now, Dolly and the rest of the staff were in the drawing room with the two sisters and brother, James. He was a tall, imposing man with a deep, cultured voice. "As you know my sister's passing will mean profound changes for us all. We, as a family, and you who served her so faithfully and well."   The staff exchanged apprehensive glances.

James went on, " Sadly we shall now be closing the house. It will be sold along with the furnishings." Dolly felt a wave a sadness sweep over her. Mrs Markham's life was in this house. Now it would go to strangers. The man raised his hands apologetically. "Unfortunately that will mean the end of your employment here. We will ask you to continue to maintain the household until the sale is complete. Then you will each receive three months wages and let go." He looked at the crestfallen faces around him. "Needless to say you will each be given a splendid reference which I am sure will go a long way in ensuring you obtain another post."

Eunice Webb stood up. "My sister and I echo my brother's sentiments and thank you for your service. In the interim period Miss Deans will act as the head of the household in our place. She will have full authority until the sale."

Each of the staff muttered their thanks and left. In the hallway they all hugged and shed tears. Making their way to the kitchen Martha made them all cups of hot sweet tea. They were lost in profound sadness of Edith Markham's passing. But now all, including Dolly, dreaded an uncertain future.

Chapter Thirty

She could not believe she was closing the door for the last time. Never again would Dolly step into the house. The past month had been both wearying and sad. She had worked hard to make sure all Mrs Markham's affair were in order as far as she could. Her employer's interests were extensive and Dolly had to contact countless organisations and societies appraising them of the situation.

The atmosphere in the house was muted during that time. Dolly and the others spoke to each other in hushed tones and moved around almost on tip-toe. The last week had been the most distressing as men from the auction house began to do an inventory, sticking labels everywhere. Dolly Deans felt angry, thinking it was affront to Mrs Markham's memory.

The staff had left earlier. Dolly had taken a last walk around the silent house. As she reached the front door she turned. "Goodbye, ma'am" she said softly before stepping outside. Walking down the stairs she strode quickly away. She could not bear to look back. After waiting a few moments she caught a tram to Trafalgar Square Almost the last entry in Mrs Markham's social diary was a NUWSS march in the square for that day.

While she was not in the right frame of mind for demonstrating she felt she should go as a last act of respect to Mrs Markham. As the tram rattled and rocked along she opened her bag and took out the little ceramic bell Edith Markham had used when she wanted tea served. Dolly had asked the family is she might have it as a memento. They readily agreed. She shook the little bell gently. The soft tinkle evoked so many memories. The first time she had visited from Wentlock's. The countless afternoons over tea and crumpets when she would tell Mrs Markham all her loves, hopes and fears. The fun. The laughter.

The ding of the tram bell jerked her out of her reverie. The conductor called out 'Trafalgar Square.' Jumping off she mingled with a crowd of about a thousand women, all wearing NUWSS sashes and some carrying banners. Dolly joined the parade as they marched around the square calling for the vote for women.

Some men watching called out abusively but Dolly held her head high. She was doing this march for Mrs Markham. Afterwards Millicent Fawcett gave a stirring speech as she stood between two of the lions at the base of Nelson's Column. With a final flourish of hurrahs they dispersed.

On the tram back to Whitechapel Dolly took a little watch from the top pocket of her blouse. She had bought it some weeks ago after becoming tired of always having to look through shop windows or up at buildings to know the time.

As the conveyance made its way east Dolly turned over in her mind what her future options might be. In many ways her situation was more complicated than the rest of staff. Their choices would be straight forward, more of the same kind of work. But Dolly Deans realised she was now a 'tweeny,' a term used for those who were caught between upstairs and downstairs. In her work for Mrs Markham she was not seen as a servant, but neither was she an equal, in the social sense.

One thing Dolly knew that she could not go back to shop work or the other types of drudge tasks that were the usual choices for girls of her class. Mrs Markham had opened her horizons, given her skills and ambitions. The thought of being subjected to petty tyrants like Miss Meredith again was unthinkable. Perhaps, she thought, with her mastery of book-keeping and typewriting she might find work in an office.

Then her thoughts turned to her first love, teaching. Miss Burgess had written to her a couple of weeks ago saying she had information concerning the education charity. Dolly had been too swamped with sorting out Mrs Markham's affairs to give it any thought, but now the offer was more tempting.

Arriving in Whitechapel she made her way to her old school. Walking through the gates, memories came flooding back. In her mind's eye she saw herself and Millie skipping rope and playing hopscotch. Thomas, kicking a football or running around acting the fool.

Stepping inside the smell, too, was evocative of those days. She made her way along the corridor, looking through the glass panels at the students. One or two of the teachers she knew were still there and waved.

Knocking on Miss Burgess' door a voice told her briskly to enter. The head-teacher beamed when she saw Dolly. " Well, now, Miss Dolly Deans, how lovely to see you. Sit down," she said, indicating a chair.

While she sat down Miss Burgess called outside for two teas. Sitting behind her desk she said, "Well now, Miss Deans, what's been happening and what brings you here?" Dolly gave the teacher a brief outline of what had happened in the last few weeks. The older woman shook her head sadly. "That is so tragic. I'm very sorry, Dolly. I know you were very close to the poor lady."

At that moment the school secretary came in and placed two cups on the desk. Miss Burgess resumed. "So, now, I take it you might be in a position to consider training to be a teacher." Dolly nodded. "You know it's always a dream of mine, Miss Burgess. But up to now circumstances have been against it." She took a sip of tea. ""Now it's something I would like to seriously consider again."

Miss Burgess smiled. "Good. Good." She took a file from a drawer. " I think you fulfil all the criteria for the grant. I can see no problems. The only thing which might prove difficult is the amount they give. Only eighteen shilling a week during training. Of course that improves dramatically when you qualify."

The younger woman's heart sank. Eighteen shillings? It was less than she got at Wentlock's. And much less than her salary with Mrs Markham. Almost as if she could read her thoughts Miss Burgess said, "I realise that this stipend is very modest. But I hope you can find some way to take up this offer, Dolly. You would make a wonderful teacher."

Dolly Deans stood up. "Thank you, Miss Burgess for all the trouble you've taken. I will think about things. When do I have to let the charity know?" The head-teacher smiled. "The training would start in September. So you have plenty of time still."

On the walk home Dolly's mind was in a turmoil. The thought that she might again lose the chance to teach was devastating. It would have been the perfect move after recent events. But if she took the training grant it would mean the family would once again be reduced to scrimping and scraping. It seemed fate was determined to thwart her dreams at every turn.

The one small comfort was that she had been paid three months wages so for the short term she and the family would be alright. Reaching the front steps she was so preoccupied that she walked past without noticing Old Peggy's Dog, who was wagging his tail in expectation. Stepping into the living room she found her mother with tears running down her face.

"Mum, what's wrong," she asked anxiously. Mrs Deans stifled a sob. "It's Billy, he's been arrested."

Chapter Thirty One

Thomas held her hand. "That's all I could find out at the station so far. " Dolly looked at him despairingly. "But Billy's no thief, Thomas, you know that." The young policeman shrugged helplessly. " I know, but from what I was told he was caught in the act."

Dolly shook her head in despair. After all the recent heartaches now this. She looked steadily at Thomas, "You know what Hannah Pemberton is, everyone in Whitechapel knows. Can the police really take her word against Billy's?"

Holding her close he said "Of course not. We all know what Hannah Pemberton is up to, but proving it is another matter. On the surface all the evidence is against him. The Pemberton woman says he snatched money from the counter and ran out. People at the tram stop heard her shout stop thief and grabbed Billy. He had the money in his hand."

"So what happens now?" Dolly asked anxiously. "Well, he'll be taken to magistrates court charged and then remanded for trial." "Remanded? Remanded where?" Thomas squeezed her hand. "Prison, I'm afraid. " Dolly let out a whimper of despair. "Prison? He's only fifteen."

**

The grey, granite walls of the prison caused Dolly's spirits to sink even lower. It had been three weeks since Billy had been sent there to await trial. During that period the matter had been the talk of Whitechapel. Most people suspected that anything involving Hannah Pemberton was to be taken with a pinch of salt. But she also knew there were a few who thought that Dolly Deans was getting a bit above herself and took a spiteful satisfaction at Billy's arrest.

After she had been sitting half an hour in a grim waiting room, filled with other visitors, a warder ushered them into a large chamber, It was divided in two by a heavy wire screen. The prisoners sat on one side, family members on the other.

When she saw Billy, Dolly almost cried. He looked thin and frightened. A little boy in a terrible place. She put on a brave face, smiling cheerfully. Dolly knew the last thing her brother needed was a depressing visit. She also needed to be calm. It was important to get his side of the story for the first time. "How are you, Billy?" she asked. The boy tried a brave smile. "Oh, you know, sis, this place is a home from home." Dolly could see tears were not far away. "Mum and Liza send their love. Liza keeps asking for you."

There was a moment of silence then Dolly leaned forward, lowering her voice. " Tell me what happened, Billy. Tell me the whole truth." He looked at her. "I swear I didn't steal that money, sis. Mrs Pemberton gave it to me," he said with a tremor in his voice.

Dolly looked at her brother. She knew him. He was telling the truth. "She *gave* it to you?" Billy nodded vigorously several times. "Yes, I swear it's true, Dolly. I was walking past the shop and Mrs Pemberton called me in, said she needed to pay Mellors, the hardware shop in Vallance Road, before they closed or they would not deliver the next day."

The boy struggled to fight back tears. " She said if I got there in time she would give me half a crown. That's why I was running. But just as soon as I set off I heard her shouting stop thief. That's when I got arrested. Mrs Pemberton told the policeman I'd run into the shop and snatched the bag of money."

Sitting back in the chair Dolly tried to work out why Hannah Pemberton would do this to her brother. "Did you upset her at any time, just before this happened?" "No," Billy said vehemently. "Not a thing, I swear."

Lowering her voice, speaking distinctly and slowly she said. "Now, Billy, she must have had a reason to do this, so you must really, really think hard." His brow furrowed in concentration. "No, nothing... Except..." His sister's voice grew urgent. "Except?"

"A few days ago, little Ernie Woods and Sid Green told me Mrs Pemberton had asked them in and told them about a big house in Poplar that was empty, the people were away. She said it was easy to get in. If they broke in and

299

brought her any jewellery she would give them lots of money."

"What did you say?" "Well," Billy said, with a shake of his head, "Ernie's only eleven and Sid's twelve. I told them not to think of robbing the house. Told them they would end up in jail. Then I said if they didn't forget about it I'd tell their mum and dad."

Dolly knew immediately why Hannah Pemberton had fabricated the crime. She had learned of Billy's interjection. So, it was partly revenge, and partly to show the rest of Whitechapel what would happen to anyone interfering with her plans. She was appalled at sheer cold-heartedness of a woman who would send a young boy to prison for years, just as a warning to others.

The bell rang for the end of visiting hours. Dolly touched Billy's fingers through the wire mesh. "Billy, don't worry, somehow, someway I'll get you out of here."

*

Hannah Pemberton looked at Dolly mockingly as she came into the shop. Pemberton was a tall, angular woman, with gaunt features and her hair tied back in a tight bun.

"What can I do for you, Miss Deans. Some pots and pans? A new washing board perhaps?" she said in a sneering tone. Dolly ignored her insolent manner. "You know why I'm here, Mrs Pemberton. It's about my brother." The tall woman affected a sympathetic sigh. "Ah, yes, what a pity. To see one so young go down the wrong path. I do what I can through my charities but there are always bad apples."

It was all Dolly could do to keep her temper. But she knew Billy's fate rested with this woman so when she spoke it was in a calm and conciliatory manner. "Mrs Pemberton, we both know Billy is innocent. I know you have your reasons for what you've done. Now everyone knows your power. You've taught us all a lesson about interfering in your business. But I'm asking you, pleading with you, to let this matter drop." Dolly held out her hands in in appeal. "Please, don't destroy my brother's life. Our family will never come near you again. Just show some forgiveness."

302

The shop-keeper chuckled unpleasantly. "I am not in the business of forgiveness, Miss Deans, I am in the business of making money. Now, if you do not wish to buy anything please leave."

Dolly was about to speak but could see nothing she could say further would move Pemberton. She turned and walked from the shop.

Chapter Thirty Two

"Phew" Thomas said the next day as Dolly told him the whole story. The young policeman looked astounded. "I knew the Pemberton woman was bad, but to do that to a young boy." Dolly looked at him hopefully. "Now that we know what she's up to we must be able to do something, Thomas."

He shook his head helplessly. "Not without proof." Dolly's voice rose in anger. "But she all but admitted what she's done. Surely I can give evidence?" The young policeman grimaced. "She might have hinted but she did not actually admit doing it. And even if she did it would only be hearsay. Your word against hers, Dolly." He held her close. "No, the only way we can get her is to have her admit the crime to the police or in front of witnesses."

**

Dolly and Millie sat in the back room of the bakery. They had been there for more than an hour going over what had happened to Billy. "What about the two boys she tried to get to rob the house? Couldn't they give evidence?" Millie asked. Her friend sighed. "Even if they agreed, which I doubt, they would be torn to pieces in the witness box."

Millie Ryan got up and poured them both another cup of tea. "Would you like a sandwich, Dolly?" Her friend declined with a shake of the head. "What was it Thomas said were the only ways to catch her out, again?" " Either she confesses or witnesses hear her admit it."

Dolly went on. "Fat chance of any of those things happening. She's too cunning for that." A slow smile crossed Millie's face. "Well, this is Whitechapel and we're Whitechapel girls. If two Whitechapel girls can't out-cunning Hannah Pemberton then my name aint Millie Ryan and yours aint Dolly Deans."

Chapter Thirty Three

Dolly and Millie stood in the doorway of a building a few doors along from the Pemberton's shop, on the opposite side of the road. Turning to her friend Dolly asked "Are you sure you want to do this, Millie?" "Well, it was your idea. Have you thought of a better one?" "No." said Dolly. "Well then, you keep out of sight and I'll go and hook the fish." With a wink she hurried across the High Street.

Hannah Pemberton looked around as shop bell jangled. Millie stepped up to the counter, The angular shopkeeper gave a thin-lipped smile. "Can I help you?" Millie Ryan looked around. "You sell a lot of nice stuff here." "Thank you," Pemberton said uncertainly. Her customer leaned on the counter. "I hear you buy stuff as well as sell it?" The tall woman looked guardedly at her. "Buy stuff?"

Millie grinned. "Nice stuff. I've heard you buy nice stuff." Hannah Pemberton frowned. "Nice stuff? What sort of nice stuff?" The younger woman leaned forward and spoke in a low voice." Gold stuff." The shopkeeper looked at her keenly. She knew Millie from seeing her around Whitechapel. Cautiously she said, "Everyone likes gold if the price is right. What sort of gold are we talking about?"

Looking around with exaggerated caution Millis lowered her voice. "Two gold rings, a gold watch. Twenty four carat. How much?" Pemberton appraised her shrewdly through half-closed eyes. "I'd have to see the merchandise first. Bring them round the back of the shop about ten tonight." Millie shook her head negatively. "No, you come to my place instead." The tall woman looked surprised. "Why not here?" "Because I like to do things where I'm comfortable. I feel safer on home territory."

Hannah Pemberton waved her away. "Then I'm sorry. I don't do business that way."

Millie made for the door. "Oh, well such a pity. The goods will bring a very good profit. But if you don't want to do business at my place, then there's plenty in Whitechapel who will."

As she pulled the door open the bell jangled loudly. Suddenly Hannah Pemberton called out.

"Wait." She walked over and looked hard at Millie. "Alright, I will come, but, I warn you, you had better not be wasting my time."

Giving her the address Millie made her way along the High Street where she joined her friend. "Well?" Dolly asked expectantly. Millie Ryan winked. "She took the bait. Now we have some arrangements to make before we reel her in."

**

The clock in Whitechapel High Street struck ten. Millie sat in the back room and went over in her head what they had planned. At that moment she heard a soft tapping at the back door of the bakery. She hurried over and drew back the

310

bolts. Pulling the door open she ushered Hannah Pemberton inside.

Her visitor had a face like thunder and ignored Millie's cheerful greeting. "Have a seat, Mrs Pemberton. Would you like a piece of cake?" Pemberton scowled at her. "I did not come here to socialise or eat cake. I'm a busy woman. Now, do you have goods to sell or not?" "Alright. No need to be snappy, just trying to make you comfortable said Millie." Hannah Pemberton 's voice rose. "I warn you, missy, if you brought me here to waste my time it will be the worse for you." Millie held out her hands in a placatory gesture. "Sorry."

Opening a table drawer she took out a little handkerchief. She opened it to reveal a gold watch and two rings. They gleamed in the lamplight. Pemberton picked them up and appraised them with a critical eye for couple of moments. Turning to Millie she said, "Not top quality but I will buy them. Three pounds."

Millie let out as sharp bark of laughter. "Three pounds? Are you joking? That lot is worth ten if it's worth a penny." The shopkeeper sneered. "Three pounds, take it or leave it." Millie Ryan covered the gold back up in the handkerchief. "Then I'll leave it."

Hannah Pemberton's face became a mask of rage. "You waste my time. Take what I offer or I warn you I will make you very sorry. You know my reputation, so that is not an idle threat."

Millie looked at her. "Oh you mean like you did with Billy Deans?"

The woman bared her teeth in a nasty grin. "You know about that?" The young baker shrugged. "Everyone in Whitechapel knows." Pemberton stepped closer. "Then you know he crossed my path and so I made up a little story about him robbing my shop. He'll have a lot of years in prison to regret interfering with my business." Millie looked at her in disbelief. "You mean you lied to send a young boy to prison, just like that?" "Yes, and I could do the same for you if you don't take the money offered."

At that point the store-room door swung open. Out stepped Dolly, Thomas and another man. Pemberton turned and looked wildly at the trio.

"What is this? Who are these people?" The man, dressed in civilian clothes, stepped forward. "I am Sergeant O'Hara of the detective force. This is police constable Turner. Hannah Pemberton I am placing you under arrest on the charge of perverting the course of justice."

The arrested woman stared in outraged disbelief. "This...this is scandalous. I've been tricked." "You can keep that for the court, Pemberton." Sergeant O'Hara said curtly. Looking balefully at the smiling Dolly and then at Millie she realised who had trapped her. Giving them both a hateful stare she shouted. "I will pay you back for this. That's a promise." As the sergeant led her away she turned and pointed at Millie. "What about her, officer, you must arrest her too. She has stolen goods"

Millie picked up the watch and rings. "Stolen? These belong to my old mum and dad."

Chapter Thirty Four

As Billy stepped out the gates of the prison Liza ran to meet him. He hugged his little sister tight and then in turn held his mother and Dolly. There were tears in Mrs Deans eyes. "Oh, Billy, we were so worried. You could have been locked up for years and years and years."

Smiling at his mother he said, "But I'm out, thanks to sis and Millie." Dolly dried her own eyes. It had been a terrible few weeks but now the Deans family were together again.

On the omnibus home Billy turned to Dolly. "How did you think of what you did to trap Pemberton?" His sister grinned. "Well, when me and Millie Ryan get together anything's possible."

Back at the house Dolly and her mother had prepared a lovely dinner for Billy. After the poor food in the prison he had lost weight. As they tucked into a thick stew Dolly said, "Oh, by the way, Thomas told me that after her arrest the police searched the shop. In the basement they found a whole lot of stolen property. Hannah Pemberton won't see Whitechapel for a long time."

There was a knock at the door. Dolly let Millie in. She had, as usual, brought cakes for the family. As she joined them at their meal. Mrs Deans looked at Dolly and her friend. "That was so clever what you girls did. So clever. But how did you get the police involved?"

Dolly mopped up the gravy in her plate with a piece of bread. "I told Thomas and he went and saw Sergeant O'Hara. He's been after Hannah Pemberton for a long time, but could never find enough evidence. He jumped at the chance to arrest her."

When the meal was over they all sat around the table enjoying the eclairs Millie had brought. Liza's hands and face were covered in chocolate and cream. Mrs Deans looked severely at Billy. "Now, William Deans. The only reason this happened is because you wander around Whitechapel with too much time on your hands. Tomorrow you're going right out and finding a proper job!"

Her son's eyes widened in outrage. "That aint fair, mum. You know I've been looking for a proper job for months." "What sort of job you looking for? " Millie asked, chipping in. "Anything steady, but what I'd really like is a trade." " A trade?" Millie continued, "what sort of trade?"

Wiping the chocolate off Liza's forehead Billy said, "Any trade. If you've got a trade you'll always earn a living. That's what dad always said." "How would you like to be a baker?" The boy looked at Millie in astonishment. "A baker? Me?" She laughed. "It's a trade aint it? One thing about being a baker, you'll never go hungry. And in the winter when everyone's shivering you'll be cosy and warm."

Dolly clapped her hands in excitement. "Millie, that's a wonderful idea." Turning to her brother she said, "Billy, you take this chance, you'll never get another one like it" The boy beamed. "Yes, please, Millie, And thank you ever so much."

Millie Ryan patted him on the shoulder. "Monday morning four o'clock, don't be late." The family all congratulated him. The mood at the table was sublime. As Dolly started to clear the dishes her brother turned to Millie. "Here, Millie, do I get to eat any of the cakes that fall on the floor?"

*

When the family had gone to bed Dolly sat staring into the fire. She was very tired. The past few weeks had taken their toll both physically and mentally. The passing of Mrs Markham had broken her heart and then the awful fear for Billy had compounded the strain.

Leaning back in the chair she at last had time to contemplate her own future. The three months wages would give her some breathing room at least. But she needed to find employment that not only paid reasonably well but would allow her to use what she had learned, taking comfort in the fact that her worries about Billy were now over. It was wonderful of Millie to take him on. Dolly felt lucky to have such a good friend.

A half-thought had been floating around her mind about possible employment. When Mrs

Markham had brought Miss Davis from her solicitor's office to teach her the typewriter, the secretary had told her she obtained jobs from an employment agency in the west end which specialised in office workers. She had given Dolly the name and address As she began to nod sleepily from the heat of the fire Dolly decided in the morning she would call and see if she could obtain a post

Chapter Thirty Five

"Thank you so much, Miss Deans. We have all your details,. There is nothing on our books today for book-keeping or typists, but opportunities come in daily. So if you'd care to call again tomorrow ,or any other time, we may have something for you." Dolly muttered her thanks and made her way out of the office. The lady behind the desk had been kind and helpful. After studying the curriculum vitae, written out in her best copperplate, the receptionist sounded positive.

But Dolly would have preferred to be offered a position there and then. The idea of calling back and forth until something turned up was not what she needed. With each week that passed her options diminished. The salary she received when she left the Markham house was slowly shrinking. If she did not get a post before it was gone she was faced with the dreadful prospect of going back to low-paid drudge work.

She also had the option of teacher-training, but the low income would make that really difficult, although with Billy now earning not impossible.

On the journey back home she thought of Thomas. He had been back on the beat for a few weeks. She was always thrilled to see how impressive and handsome he looked strolling along the High Street.

Getting on the tram she made her way home. On the High Street she stopped at the butcher's and bought a bone for Old Peggy's Dog. As she approached he lifted his paw. Dolly smiled. "You know just what to do, don't you Old Peggy's Dog? Here you are." Throwing him the bone she left the little mongrel happily gnawing away.

Coming into the house she found her mother bathing Liza in a tin bath. The toddler splashed the water and laughed as it soaked her mother. "Hello mum, hello naughty imp." She called across to the duo. Her mother looked at her hopefully. "Any luck love?"

Dolly shook her head. "They say perhaps. I should just keep trying. Want me to start dinner?" "Yes please, love." As Dolly moved to the sink her mother said, "By the way, there's a letter for you. Just came an hour ago." "For me?" Dolly said picking up an envelope from the table. It was of good quality paper and had some sort of embossed crest in one corner. She took a knife and slit it open. At the top of the page was the heading Hawkins, Hawkins and Hawkins. It was from Mrs Markham's solicitor. For a brief moment of panic she thought that maybe the three months salary had been a mistake.

However as she read down the page relief gave way to curiosity. Dolly was requested to attend their offices at ten o'clock the following Monday. She showed the letter to her mother. Mrs Deans brow wrinkled in puzzlement. "I wonder what it could be?" "Don't know, mum. Maybe they need some information about the accounts." "Perhaps," her mother said, "but in my

326

experience no good comes from lawyers' letters."

**

It felt to Dolly that a whole swarm of butterflies were doing a mad dance in her stomach. Since the letter from the solicitor she had been on tenterhooks as to why she had been summoned. Her mum's repeated dire warnings about no good coming of lawyers letters did not help.

It was actually a relief when it came time for the meeting. At least she would know the worst. Checking the address on the letter she found an entrance with a brass plate stating it was the offices of Hawkins, Hawkins and Hawkins. Stepping inside she told the young woman at the front desk her name and showed her the letter.

Dolly was given directions to an office on the first floor. A glass panel on the door said Mr J.W. Hawkins.

She timidly tapped and a voice from within told her to enter. Dolly stared in amazement. The room was crowded. As well as Mrs Markham's siblings, Martha, Elsie and Annie sat there, all done up in their Sunday best. They smiled and waved. Behind the desk Mr Hawkins gave her a frosty smile. "Good morning, Miss Deans. Please take a seat."

She sat beside Martha. The solicitor cleared his throat. "We are here to read the last will and testament of Edith, Euphemia Markham." Dolly and the cook exchanged smiles at the middle name. Hawkins went on. "I, Edith Euphemia

Markham etcetera state that my estate shall be divided equally among my siblings, except for the following minor bequests. To Martha Woodley, who served me faithfully and well as cook and house-keeper I leave the sum of two hundred and fifty pounds." There was an audible delighted gasp of disbelief from Martha. Dolly squeezed her arm in congratulation.

The lawyer continued, "To Elsie and Annie, I leave to each the sum of one hundred and fifty pounds." The two girls looked at each other stunned. "And to Dolly Deans, my private secretary and dear friend, I leave the sum of five hundred pounds."

*

As they sat around the table in the little café the happy quartet could still hardy believe what had just happened. Dolly felt like she should pinch herself to make sure it wasn't all a dream. After the news she had insisted they all go for lunch at her expense. She thought it only right as she had benefitted the most.

"Who would have thought it? "Martha said, spreading butter thickly on a piece of bread. "Mrs Markham, such a lovely lady and now she's made us all millionaires." At this the others laughed. The four women were all bathed in a glow of happiness. The money had ensured that they did not have any financial worries in the immediate future.

Looking at the housekeeper Dolly said, "Have you any plans for what you're going to do now, Martha?" The woman beamed. "I'm going home. To Devon." "Do you still have family there?" Dolly asked. Beaming even wider the older woman said, "Bless you, Dolly, dozens and dozens." At this they all laughed again. " When we were little my sister and I used to say how we'd like to have a tea-room, just by the sea."

She sighed blissfully. "Always our dream, it was. Now, I'm going to open that tea-room. I shall do the baking and my sister shall serve the tables. And every morning when I wake up I shall see the ocean and not the chimney pots of London."

This made them all chuckle. Dolly turned to Elsie and Annie. "And you two wealthy young ladies, what will you do with the money?" "Me," Annie said, blushing slightly, "and my young man will be able to marry." They all made sounds of delight and congratulated the red-face girl. "What of you, Elsie?" Dolly asked .The young cook smiled. "I will buy some nice things and give the rest to my mother and father." Martha patted her on the shoulder. "Good girl."

The housekeeper turned to Dolly. "And you, Dolly, what will you do with the windfall?" Dolly shook her head. "I'm not quite sure yet, Martha. But one thing I do know, I will never have to put up with the Miss Merediths of this world again."

Chapter Thirty Six

"Is this really mine?" Mrs Deans said wonderingly as she looked around the room. "Yes, mum," Dolly retorted , spreading her arms expansively, "all yours." Her mother stood almost in a daze while Liza ran up and down the hallway.

Dolly had thought long and hard about the best way to use her inheritance. She knew it was a lot of money but not enough to keep them forever. So she decided that she would firstly buy a little house for the family, away from the shabby, tumbledown place they lived.

It was near the original area they had resided in before her father's passing. In a quiet cul-de-sac, far removed from the bustle and roar of

Whitechapel High Street, the house had a little back garden, perfect for Liza to play in. It had cost two hundred pounds. But for Dolly it was well worth the money. It would give her family a safe roof over their heads, no longer at the mercy of a landlord who kept raising the rent.

She then carefully worked out the most advantageous way to use the rest. One unexpected avenue was to invest some of it in Millie's business. Her friend's shop was thriving and she was already planning to open another one in two or three year's time.

When they discussed this Dolly suggested she buy a share in the venture. Millie was delighted, It would let her forge ahead at a faster pace. It was agreed that Mrs Deans would be paid a small percentage of the profits every week. Dolly was happy that this, coupled with Billy's wage, it would mean her mother and Liza would be comfortable. It also meant that she could accept the teacher training salary without causing hardship. The remainder would go towards her and Thomas' future.

With Liza and her mother, Dolly Deans made her way back to Whitechapel. Mrs Deans spoke excitedly about buying furniture. When they reached the entrance to their building Old Peggy's Dog was sitting on the steps. The little dog was not his usual energetic self. He did not jump up when Dolly appeared.

She had not seen him for a few days and he looked thinner. She patted his head, while Liza stroked him. "What's the matter, Old Peggy's Dog? Are you sick?" At that moment Mrs Munday, one of their neighbours, came out. "Poor little thing." "Why, what's happened? Dolly asked. The woman looked down at the little dog. "Peggy was taken poorly. So her daughter took her off to live with her in Essex."

Ruffling the mongrel behind the ears Dolly asked "But what about the dog?" Mrs Munday shrugged, "Daughter didn't want it I sp'ose." Looking at the sad little canine Dolly Deans turned to her mother. "Mum, we can't leave him here. We have to take him with us."

At that moment Liza threw her arms around the dog's neck. Mrs Deans sighed in good-natured resignation. "How can we not, now?"

The little girl squealed with delight. Dolly scratched Old Peggy's Dog behind the ears. "Come on, bow-wow, welcome to the family."

***

Dolly stood by the graveside, a bunch of flowers in her hand. She had not been to Mrs Markham's grave since the funeral. But now she wanted to say a final farewell and a final thanks to the woman who had changed her life

Edith Markham had treated her kindness and respect. Had given her skills and had opened a wider world up to her. Dolly knew just how much she owed her. She placed the flowers on the grave. Wiping away a tear she said. "Goodbye, ma'am, I'll always carry a little place for you in my heart.

Chapter Thirty Seven

Frost dappled the back garden as Dolly looked out. It was Christmas Eve. Her mother came into the room carrying her daughter's wedding dress. "Nice and pressed and not a wrinkle," she called out cheerfully. The bride-to-be shot her a smile of thanks. "It looks beautiful, mum. The best dress you've ever made." She took the gown from her mother and slipped it on. Turning and facing Mrs Deans she said. "How do I look, mum?"

Tears started in the older woman's eyes and for a few seconds she could not speak. When she did her voice was husky with emotion. "Oh, Dolly, you look like a princess, love. Your dad would have been so proud of you." Mother and daughter hugged. At that moment Millie walked in. "Now, ladies, no time for the waterworks. There's a groom waiting and that little flower girl downstairs is eating all the petals."

Mrs Deans rolled her eyes. "That girl will be the death of me." She rushed out. Millie looked at Dolly. "You look a sight for sore eyes, Dolly Deans. Thomas Turner's a lucky man." "Thanks, Millie." She took her friends hand. "And thanks again." Millie's brow furrowed. "Thanks again? What does that mean? "Thanks again for being such a great friend. I don't know if I could have got through this year without you."

Millie waved away the compliment. "Get a move on, the carriage will here in a minute." She left but then popped her head back round the door. "Oh, and don't forget to thank Thomas for choosing such a handsome best man. He's a real bobby dazzler." She winked and disappeared from sight.

Dolly grinned. Thomas' best man was one of his friends from the force. Tall and handsome as Millie asked. She checked her hair in the mirror one last time and thought so much had happened in so short a time and now here she was about to marry the man she loved.

Many people were surprised that she had chosen this time of year but Dolly always loved Christmas. It was a time of so much happiness when her father was alive and all the Deans were together. Her choice was a little homage to her dad's memory.

With a final check she took a deep breath and walked through the door.

*

The organ played the wedding march as the newly-married bride and groom walked up the aisle. Those lining each side smiled. Dolly and Thomas made such a perfect couple. He was tall and handsome and she was radiantly lovely. It was obvious to all how deeply in love they were.

As she passed her mother and Liza, her little sister blew her kiss. Billy, wearing a smart suit, looked very grown up. He winked at Dolly. Reaching the front door of the church the young couple both looked in wonder as the snow floated down gently. It was the perfect Christmas wedding.

Thomas leaned close and whispered "Merry Christmas, Mrs Turner." Dolly stood on tiptoe and kissed him gently on the cheek. "Merry Christmas, Mr Turner."

THE END.

Printed in Great Britain
by Amazon

.